IT
IS NOT MY GIRLFRIEND

AJITH SIVA

ELYSIAN
Imprints

It is not my girlfriend
Ajith Siva

It is not my girlfriend
Ajith Siva

This is a work of fiction. Names, characters, places, and incidents either are the product of the author's imagination or are used fictitiously. Any resemblance to actual persons, living or dead, events, or locales is entirely coincidental.

Copyright © 2022 by Ajith Siva
All rights reserved.

No part of this book may be reproduced or used in any manner without the written permission of the copyright owner except for the use of quotations in a book review.

First Published in Feb 2022
Typeset in Cardo 10

Cover design by Ajith Siva

Proofreading by Lakshana Jyothi

ISBN 9798416284794

To surf: www.ajithsiva.home.blog
To write: ajithsivawrites@gmail.com
To follow: Instagram.com\ajithsiva_author

This was just another draft turned into a book when your hands touched it before your eyes could see.
You complete me, Thank you!

We each have three faces.

The first face, you show to the world.
The second face, you show to your close friends and family.
The third face, you never show anyone.
It is the truest reflection of who you are.

—Unknown

— Prologue —

Her father is an underrated poet. When he held her for the first time, the abundance of melanin in her body made her eyeballs thick and dark. He could only come up with one name, and that is Karuvizhi. Karu's eyes are black as night oceans. No one can read her mind as it is enclosed with the noises of the ocean. She is the mystery of this story.

Aaron and Karu are peculiar to all other soulmates. They had never called each other by pet names, they had never had long phone calls, they had never spent extra time in cafes after dining, and they had never walked in the rain together. Even in their walk in a good climate, Karu had to run to match his normal speed. He hadn't grabbed her hands unless they were crossing roads. Most of the time silence was their other companion. He hadn't asked her to marry him. It was an unsaid pact that they knew each other.

For his whole life, Aaron never knew when he started to love Karu. It was always her from the beginning. From the day when he heard her name, the 'lee' sound in this name is pronounced as 'zhi'. From the first day, he was ready to turn back and face the heat from her eyes. From the day she wished for his 12th birthday with a smile on the corner of her lips. For him, the moment of love started was remembered as a memory. Or a dream.

Aaron had asked Karu if she had a dream of them together. It was when they both were sitting on the shore, her hairs were waving along with the oceans in the wind. She was thinking deep, her eyeballs ironically reflecting the oceans in crystal clear. Aaron or no one could say what was inside her mind. She had one. A long time ago in her blurred dream, she was alone and watching Aaron playing with their kids in a beautiful place. She had never thought about the dream after that. She wished that to happen as late as it could take. She had the patience to wait for everything. And she felt that would be everything. That would be the only happy ending she wished to have.

Aaron didn't get the answer he asked. Their minds were never on the same page. Their stories too. Coincidentally, they happened to be in the same place.

Elysia was announced as Elysian City at the time people from different cultures and races came to live. Aaron is this city's boy. During school, he enjoyed a few extra local holidays even though he didn't have to celebrate them. The other thing that happened to him in school was Karu. Aaron's family and Karu's family came from two different poles. But they both ended up studying in the same school located between the same distances from both of their houses.

In his memory or dream, they both were 17, Karu was a little girl with double side braided hair who he met every day. One fine evening, she was sitting there in front of him and looking at him. He was not sure if she was looking at him or not. But he knew he looked straight into her eyes. It was the black that has surrounded the universe. Those two black eyeballs were gleaming a universe.

That was the time, Aaron realized how suitable the name she has. The time he fell for the gravity in her eyes. He wrote her name with his name on the first page of his notebook. The storm from her eyes passed through him and swirled in his adolescent nerves. He was in the storm for a while. It flipped the pages to the last like there it was written that she is the one who was born for him. That's where the crush turned into love. He doesn't remember much about what he saw inside that universe. He knew it was a prophecy. A moment that will happen in time.

What is that prophecy? Who opened that universe? Why did her ocean become calm for him? Who or what made this all happen?

Let's call it by the current phenomenon "The Universe." The Universe created its first eye 541 million years ago in some organism. It was the time it wanted to see things and to see itself. So, the Universe is seeing us and it knows what and how much one wants and how to deliver them in a way they won't forget. Sometimes the package can be a lesson too. (Most of the time they are lessons.)

It's nothing big. People say we won't know the value of a thing until we lose it one day. And when we lose it we will look back at the time when we had it and feel how pathetically thoughtless we were.

That was the package sent to Aaron, dated on his 26th birthday.

—— Chapter One ——

'Happy Birthday, Aaron!'

I know that is me; Aaron Stitch and I know that today is my 26th birthday. What I don't know is why I'm traumatized to hear the first birthday wish from my girlfriend.

Trauma is triggered commonly by Déjà vu.

In a very long-term relationship, can anything be more surprising? Exactly a year ago, Aaron got a call from Karu a few minutes to April 19. He knew she was in his house then. And he already knew that she had arranged a birthday surprise waiting for him outside his room. He checked the mirror to see if he's photo ready.

This is what happens on all of Aaron's birthdays. Karu throws him a surprise and anyway Aaron has to do it too as after a week on Karu's birthday. He just keeps wishing her first and gifting something to her which she wanted and which she already knows.

In the same year, Aaron bought her a pair of earrings and lost them before her birthday. Karu was okay with that no-gift-birthday. Then after a week, Karu found the earrings when she was cleaning Aaron's room. She felt excited like she had found a treasure. So, Karu's birthday went well last year. But Aaron's?

Aaron opened the door. It was all dark in the living room. Glowing in candlelight, Karu was standing with a creamy white forest cake in her hands. 'Happy Birthday, Aaron!' she wished him with a smile on the corner of her lips.

Pop! Pop!

Edward and Stella, Aaron's younger siblings, popped the party poppers at the same time beside him from the darkness. Karu was scared as if a bomb had blasted and threw the cake in the air which ended up on Aaron's face, with candles burning on his t-shirt. And also, he was topped by snowing party papers. His mom turned on the light and all of his family except Karu was laughing at Aaron.

Karu was worried and wiped the cake on his face with the shawl. 'I'm so sorry. Are you okay? Have you burnt?'

'I'm okay,' He said with frosting on his face.

'Congratulations, son. You are 25 now.' Aaron's father, Mr. Stitch, wished him in the middle of his uncontrollable laughter. 'Edward! Stella! Get your spoons! We are eating cake on Aaron this year. A new tradition.'

This year, Aaron got a call from Karu in the evening. That was where his trauma started. She informed him that they both were going somewhere and he ought to not ask where that was. Aaron didn't want to spoil her plans.

He was driving on the way she guided him. They had already crossed out of Elysian City and the road was going up and down. Aaron had no idea where he was driving. But he enjoyed driving on an open highway and the fast turns on the bends.

'Go slow! Aaron,' Karu yelled weakly at Aaron.

Aaron said in his tenor voice, 'Come on, Karu. What is the point of having a car like this and driving slowly? And I cannot drive it fast in the city. Thanks for bringing me here.'

Karu sighed, 'Aaron, go slow. It gives me a head spin. I'm going to throw up in your car.'

'Alright, easy, easy there.' He eased down the car, 'Where is this place we are going?'

Karu was relieved from the over speed and the car became quiet enough to speak.

'You are not allowed to ask questions,' Karu said from the passenger seat. She had dressed in an olive skater and a yellow open sweater above it and her usual purple sandals. She has dusky brown shiny skin, crooked teeth, round nose, curvy chin, and little dark spots and acne marks on her cheeks. She usually wouldn't dress like that. She did for Aaron that day. And she set her hair loose instead of her regular braids. 'Now take the next left.'

Aaron glanced at the GPS in his new car. The green and black Mustang. 'Karu, for your information, there is no left here.'

'I know there is one. I have been here many times. Hey, look!' she pointed at a path between the woods, 'There it is. Turn left.'

He peered at the sand path. There was a rusted iron board saying "Two-wheelers not allowed. Beware of wild animals." He asked her, 'Where the hell this crap is going?'

Karu glared at him, 'Keep a mind on your language, Aaron.'

'Crap isn't added in the list of offensive words yet, I think,' Aaron felt the heat coming from her eyes.

'Okay, fine. I rephrase. Where is this path going, Madam?'

'Turn now. I will tell you,' Karu opened the glovebox and took off her watch.

Aaron shut the glove box and frowned at her, 'Please, don't keep your antique watch in my car. You will forget it here.'

'That happened just one time,' she wore it back. 'What is your problem?' Aaron noticed her fingers with henna. Karu never paints her nails. Instead, she applies the paste made with henna leaves. Like those fingers are dipped in orange colour and a solid circle in the centre of her palms like holding a sunrise.

He turned the car to the path which only Karu knows where it would go. 'Why did you come here many times?'

'It's our family vacation point.'

'Here?' Aaron paced the car away from the sharp branches as much as he could, 'Why is your family so different?'

'My family? What about your family? Why is your family… a sitcom family?'

'That's normal. We are not melodramatic like yours. We go on vacation to beaches and malls. Sometimes hill stations, not to some jungle at midnight.'

The car's headlight was the only light source before him. The path was covered with shredded leaves from the broken bamboo trees. There was no trace of another vehicle on the road.

'We come here in the daytime. And at least we don't drink in front of children.'

He chuckled, 'That's called liberty. Your parents don't know that. They insisted you study Computer Engineering for no reason. And you don't know how to install an OS on a computer.' Falling shaded leaves spin and reflect the light and land slowly on the windshield.

'And why did they forbid you to go for a job? To make you teach mathematics to the children in your neighbourhood? How much do you charge per head for that?'

'I'm not doing it for money. You won't understand it, Aaron. You don't even talk to your neighbours. They don't even know your parents have an elder son.'

'At least they will know if I say my last name is Stitch. Your family doesn't even have a surname.' Aaron pointed out the fact that Karu hates to talk. 'What is your surname? Karuvizhi K.' He mocked her, 'Present, Sir!'

'That is for a reason.'

Aaron tried to ignore her heat. 'I don't want your crappy historical reasons. Tell me the reason why we are here.'

She groaned, 'Ugh! I just wished to surprise you. Please let me surprise, Aaron. Will you?' She stared at him. 'Answer me. Will you?'

He felt the heat was too much to ignore. 'Fine, I'm sorry. I will not ask.'

'We reached the place. Park the car over there,' she pointed at a wood house in the middle of the forest where trees made a compound wall. He pulled over.

'We reached the place. Park the car over there.' It was her voice. Aaron replayed Karu's recorded words from his smartwatch. She glowered at him.

'I'm sorry, I won't do that again,' he turned off the engine. They both stretched their legs out. Aaron studied the wooden cabin. It's a kind of cabin that shows up in most horror movies. In which a group of teenagers goes in and never comes back. He still didn't know there are no lights around the place. The moon shone brighter than every other night of the year.

'What is this place?' He asked awkwardly.

'It's my grandfather's place. I have told you, remember? He lived alone in his cabin far away from us until he got the tumour.'

'Uh…' Aaron remembered everything she said. Still, he enjoyed scoffing at her family, 'Was your grandfather belonged to any tribe?'

That's why you don't have a surname, he wanted to add.

'No, he was a forest ranger. And no one lives here right now.'

'I can surely say that. What kind of vacations do you do here?'

'It's quite a pleasant place for a family vacation. Sometimes you have to get out of the city and live a minimal life, Aaron. And I always wanted to come with you here. You and me alone. So, I planned it tonight,' Karu turned pink, she held his arms, 'What do you think about that? Do you like my plan?'

'You are the boss,' he shrugged.

'It's your day. Tell me if you don't want to. We can go to your house.' She went to open the frunk.

'My house? Again, this year?' He chuckled. He couldn't help himself from freaking out. 'No, this sounds like a good plan. You and me alone. I think it's been so long since we did something like this.'

Karu turned on her battery lantern, 'You stay here with the car. I will clean and light up candles in a few minutes.'

Aaron felt a lurch in him, 'Why candles?'

'Oh! There is no electricity here.' She carried her things from the frunk, 'Don't worry. The climate will be chilled. You don't need a fan or an AC.'

'Chilled?' Aaron caught her carrying a box that carried a packet of long candles.

Karu stood frozen and tried to hide the box and the label of the bakery's name from him. 'Yes, chill. There! Look.' She pointed behind him.

He turned to see nothing. But a cliff below the moon looks like where wolves howl in those horror movies. 'What? Where?'

'The moon looks beautiful from here. Doesn't it?'

The cake, huh? He thought and rolled his eyes. 'Alright, I'm not seeing anything.'

'Please wait and look around. I will clean up the house. It won't take much time.' She walked to the house to start cleaning. A bunch of mosquitoes flew over her head.

Will she come back?

Karu is a fastidious person. Whenever she comes to Aaron's room, the room will be cleaned like magic. His bed would be made, the table would get organized and pens would go into the mug. His clothes will be folded. And the bookshelf will be stacked neatly. Aaron is a fast reader and he reads to make conversation. Every time he does a presentation in his office, he finishes it with a quote from the book he read. Or read a book that has an apt quote for his presentation.

Karu also reads books. But unlike Aaron, she kept it as a secret. She takes all the days in a month to finish a book.

And she doesn't finish some books because she doesn't want to end her bond with those books. She reads and doesn't talk about books to anyone. The only time she quoted a book was a poem from her mother tongue. And that is only to Aaron. She translated it for him.

You are the rays of light that hit me,

While I am the eyes which absorb;

Aaron means light, Karuvizhi means black eyes. She felt overwhelmed by this poet.

— Chapter Two —

The forest was thick and mysterious. Tall pine trees stood unmoved and untouched forever. Different tones of birds were chirping from the dark branches. The cabin was flat, small, and desaturated. Thorns bushed on the other side of the house. Despite the moss and rust on the house, it stood shining in the moonlight.

Aaron walked to the front porch. There was a swing covered with dusty newspapers. He peeled them and sat on the swing. Karu was lighting candles inside.

Aaron didn't notice it. His mind was full of expectations that soon he would be getting birthday wishes from his office mates. From his teammates to acquaintances. From his senior, Nazir in a group message. From his boss, Damian personally. On top of all, he waited for a call from someone.

It was Destiny. Aaron never had felt that much about her. She was filled in his thoughts. The last time he met her made a difference in how he was seeing her since the day they met first.

It was about 6 months ago. In his office conference room, Damian – the CEO of the SYS Marketing Executive Company- gathered a group of ten employees. Exactly 10 chairs were arranged for them, with pastries and packaged drinking water. Two of the ten people there shared the same age. Same thoughts. Same interests. And the curiosity to find out what other things are the same.

They were Aaron and Destiny. They both sat across each other on the first seats from Damian. He started his speech.

'Good morning, everyone… I know everyone is wondering why random people from this office have been gathered here. Let me explain. Once I had a mentor, my master who taught me this vertical business. Unfortunately, he was no more after a dreadful incident. Anyway, he said, 'Be surrounded by passionate people. People who can argue wisely. Believe in their idea. That will help you to make the right decision.'

'So, I chose you randomly without any hierarchy. You guys are the important people in this office. We will have meetings once a month and discuss our further events and plans for our growth. There are no complications here. Anyone can give suggestions and bring out great ideas. Are you with me on this?'

Everyone nodded.

'Okay, I know every one of you very well. Let's introduce you to each other. Shall we start with the lady here?' He pointed at Destiny.

'Hello, I'm Destiny,' she grabbed everyone's attention with her name. Destiny has fair skin and straight dark brown hair that covers her forehead. She wore a cream collared blouse tucked in navy blue high waist pants, with empty belt loops.

'Nice name,' Aaron said before realizing it.

'Thank you,' a smile sparkled under her pink lips. 'I'm a content writer. I don't have any long backstory. I'm a blog writer. This is my first serious job. And I don't have any idea how I get into this room. Thanks for letting me in.'

'That's a very down-to-earth speech. Guys, Destiny is known for her blog of predictions. Her recent blog on prediction on who would win the World Cup Soccer was on point. That caught many people's eye on her previous predictions which were true. I would say it is our luck that she chose to work as a commercial writer. Seriously, she has something gifted.'

Damian asked her, 'Would you please say anything about how you are doing it? It would be difficult I think, Miss. Destiny.'

Destiny smiled, 'I think predicting the future isn't hard. We will not have tomorrow what we hadn't yesterday. So, knowing about what we get and how we got it is difficult for me.'

Aaron had something that sounded like that to finish his introduction. But it faded away from his mind as he felt that was the right way to say it.

'Next, Gentleman, I don't want to give spoilers of your names,' He gestured at the next person.

Aaron didn't spare his concentration on others. They introduced themselves and Damian gave his excerpt on them. Like a long needle in the clock, it rotated fast and came to Nazir who was sitting next to Aaron. He stood and made his introduction. He was dressed formally. He was expecting this meeting to happen for a while. Because, as the Creative Head of the advertising team had retired, he would come to take the position by seniority. The position had a lot of benefits like unnumbered incentives apart from salary, vehicle loan, compensations for business trips, usage of membership cards in five-star hotels around the country.

Then Aaron stood and gave his introduction. He dressed formally in a beige dotted shirt tucked in his black pants. He finished his speech, 'I'm honoured to sit here with you all.'

'Well said, Aaron. Guys, let me tell you a little about Aaron. He came here as an intern and then we didn't want to lose him. He became one of our Advertising Managers. From the first day, we are grasping a great dedication and strong curiosity in him. Ask Mr. Nazir, our Sr. Advertising Manager who trained him,' He gestured at Nazir who nodded proudly.

'I see Aaron always walking here and there between technicians and clients. He never compromises at work. Believe me, I have been getting complaints from the ad designers and writers.'

'The truth to be told is even the clients couldn't compromise him,' Nazir mocked Aaron's stubborn creative control.

Damian smiled, 'Jokes apart. Now, the time has come to announce the new Creative head of the Advertising team.'

Nazir was ready to get up and shake everyone's hands. He wiped his bald head and adjusted his grey beard.

Damian announced, 'It's Aaron.'

The meeting was wrapped up and everyone kept wishing for Aaron. Like Nazir, he didn't expect he would take the position with just one year of experience. It showed how much Damian believes in him.

Destiny came to Aaron in the corridor. 'Hey!'

'Hey, Destiny?' he pointed at her.

She nodded, 'Aaron, congrats on your new position. That's big. I can see how hard you have worked to earn this.' They shook hands quickly.

'Thank you,' he grinned.

'Just thank you?' she pretended to be disappointed.

'Do you need anything else?'

Nazir came out of the conference room. His face was not like it was a few minutes before. Still, he pretended to be cheered up.

He smacked Aaron's shoulder, 'My boy, at last, you made me proud. Happy for you.' he said with a grumpy face and shook Aaron's hand. 'But you should keep doing it and deliver faster from now on.' He left his hand free and walked out.

'Heil Nazi!' Aaron saluted behind him. Destiny giggled.

'So, you were asking. What do you want then?'

'A coffee?' she asked without any choices.

'Sure, shall we go to the pantry?'

'Pantry?' she asked sceptically.

'Yeah, there is a coffee machine there.'

'Huh, look, Aaron, if you want to drink a regular coffee, you can go to the pantry. Unless, if you want to drink the best coffee in the city, come with me,' she walked into the elevator.

Aaron smiled and followed her to a cafe. For the last six months, they were drinking coffee for a while and chatting for a long time in the cafe each day after work.

Aaron took out the mobile phone and checked for the birthday messages. He couldn't see the bars.

'Karu!' he called out from the doorway, 'Why am I not getting phone signals?' He moved his phone up and down and searched for a signal.

The lantern in her hands came first from the door, glowing at Karu's face. 'Oh, I forgot to tell you. There are no mobile phone towers nearby.'

'What? What are we doing here then?'

She turned off the lantern and hung it in the doorway. 'Come with me. I will show you.'

For Aaron, that was not fair. If she had told him there would be no mobile phone service, he might have said they can go to his house. He was thinking about asking for a second chance. *How can I ask her again?*

He entered the house. It was all made of teak wood. No big couches or soft cushions to sit comfortably. A hall with two chairs facing a chimney, a bed at the corner preoccupied with the moonlight coming through the window. Another small room leads to a restroom which was newly built by Karu's father. For Karu's grandfather, it was an extravagance for this place.

What Aaron noticed first was, the place was fully lit with candles. Candles scared him. The candle which almost burnt him last year was a single one. This year it had brought its army.

Karu checked the time on her watch with a mischievous smile hidden on her lips that only Aaron could read.

There is a language that exists between soulmates. It is non-verbal. For most people, it is an unrealized one. Karu's eyes emit signals that Aaron receives. And her lip line is like a subtitle that only Aaron could read.

He grasped that it was all her plan. A plan to make herself wish him first. As she had brought him out of the city to a place without a phone signal, how could anyone else wish him?

Well played, Karu.

'Come on, Aaron, here,' she called him to the table where she had set up the cake. The table was made of the trees that belonged to the forest.

He looked at the cake. It was already melted. And shaken well in the car. The texts written on that were not human language anymore. 'Nice cake though.'

She smiled, 'I'm sorry. We can talk about this later. The time is going. Cut it now.'

He started to cut the cake and Karu wished him sharply at midnight, 'Happy birthday, Aaron!'

It flashed him a memory of last year's disaster. The air was thick. Now the heat from all the candles threatened him more than Karu's eyes. So, this was why Aaron was traumatized. And there was one thing Aaron felt for sure. *This year defeats the last year.*

—— Chapter Three ——

'What happened?' Aaron wondered at the closed café they both come to every day.

Destiny already started walking back. 'How do I know? Today, my scooter got repaired, and now this.'

Saturdays are meant for casual wear in their company. She wore an olive sleeve under a khaki cardigan tucked in buttoned white pants.

'Where are you going? I want a coffee now; we can hang out somewhere else,' Aaron suggested with a tired face. He wore a checked white and blue shirt and dark jeans.

'I have to catch the bus,' she sighed with a tired face, 'I'm leaving. Sorry, Aaron.'

'Okay, fine. I will drop you off at your house. I don't have anything to do now,' he clicked his key and unlocked the car. It beeped.

'Are you sure?' She walked next to him on the pavement.

'Yeah. And this is all your fault,' he pointed at her.

'What did I do to you to blame me?'

'You introduced me to this café. Now, my taste buds are denying office coffee.' They both got in the car.

Damn Phone Signals!

Aaron was standing in the moonlight on the front porch, looking at his phone every four minutes for a network.

'Look!' Karu walked behind him and pointed to a star she spotted falling, 'A shooting star on your birthday! Make a wish.'

He chuckled, 'Karu, it is a satellite. And also, what can a star bring me?'

'Then ask me, what do you want for this birthday?' as every year she asked.

Unusual to every year, he said, 'A coffee now?'

She was speechless. Then she said, 'Coffee? Where shall I go for a coffee?' She looked around, 'I'll buy you when we leave from here. I promise.'

Aaron is hardly a coffee lover. He hadn't had a coffee since the morning. He thought it was causing a headache. And believed it was breaking his head. *I secretly wish that Karu could have the same head pain as me then she would know how badly I need a coffee right now.*

'Ask for anything else.'

'What else I may need?'

'Think well about that,' Again, a mischievous smile glimpsed on her lips. The language of soulmates came to play.

But Aaron was not getting what she was trying. This is their traditional way of flirting with each other. On both birthdays someone would ask for wishes and they pretend to be there is nothing to ask and finally, the other one who was asked for the wish will ask for a kiss. Obviously, Aaron needs to ask Karu for a kiss right now in this game. If he doesn't ask, Karu will lose. Strange game.

'Okay, tell me. What is your favourite food?' He asked.

Karu started to think as if he had asked this for the first time. Karu has no favourite food. This is the only weirdest thing Aaron finds about her. He always wondered about this ever since they started to see each other. *How could someone live without having a favourite food? Even cats, dogs, and birds have their favourite foods,* He thought.

'I don't know,' she bent her brows and was thinking about it, 'I like whatever my mom makes me. And I like your mom's too.'

Whatever high-class restaurants Aaron brings her to, she doubts the hygiene of the food. That evening, before they took on the road, Aaron brought her to a bistro and ordered Spaghetti with meatballs. Karu was not sure about the meat's freshness. She looked for other diners' reactions. But the restaurant was empty. She asked him why.

And she didn't even touch the dessert.

Again, Aaron took out his phone and checked for a signal that wouldn't come until they leave that place. He couldn't know if he had any texts or calls or birthday wishes. His mind was phrasing questions. *What if my colleagues want to wish me? What If Des calls to wish me? What if she tries to call and can't get me?*

'Shall I play a song for you?' Karu asked. She knew that he was upset. His face said it all. But not why it was.

'Songs?' he froze his chuckle and shook his head, 'No, I just need some peace of mind.'

When it comes to songs, Aaron and Karu are always complimentary. She would sleep when he plays his favourite songs. And some of her favourite songs for him are so old that even his mom didn't know.

Destiny holds a playlist of songs similar to Aaron's favourites. After they saw the café where they used to hang out every evening was closed yesterday. They were disappointed and to kill time, Aaron offered her a ride to her home, in his new car with the newly built sound system in it.

'Wow, the sound is ripping my ears.' Destiny enjoyed the ride with open windows.

'I love this album.' He bawled.

'Really? I love this composer more than anyone can.'

'Excuse me, stop copying me. Okay?' The song changed to a melody from the same album. He reduced the volume.

She giggled and opened the glove box. 'Whose watch is this?' She took out Karu's watch.

Aaron remembered the last ride with Karu when he dropped her at the corner of her street. 'Oh, that's my mom's watch.'

'I guessed it would be your mom's,' she snapped.

'Really? How did you guess?'

'It is a bit old-fashioned. Today's girls won't wear this, I bet,' she flipped it, 'Hey! Look at the year, it is twenty-six years old. It is nearly your age. I think your mom bought this to feed you at the right time.'

'Okay, Detective Destiny. You got me,' he steered left to her street.

She placed it back in the box, 'I'm not detecting. I'm just trying to get to know you more.'

'So, how far you have got into knowing me.'

'Pretty well so far, I think.'

'Okay then, tell me something about me that I don't know.'

'Huh! I can tell you. But it will be like judging.' She shook her head.

'Okay, I will give you a guilt-free pass. Judge me.'

'Okay,' she leaned her elbow at the window and turned to him, 'You are so bad at multitasking.'

'What multi-tasking?' Aaron drove further and looked for Destiny's apartment that he should have reached by then.

'I mean you can think about only one thing at a time.'

'Everybody does this.'

'Yes, but you are the worst. While you are working on something, if someone asks you your name, you don't have an answer. At first, I thought you were enabled at work. Then I confirmed this when last week a person asked you the time and you took more time to answer him.'

'That's not true,' he denied by his head shake. 'Look, I'm driving now, listening to the lyrics and talking to you. Isn't this look like multi-tasking for you?'

'You are driving in the wrong way, Aaron. Look around.'

'Crap!' he slammed the steering wheel, 'I must turn to the next left.'

She giggled, 'Crap yourself and admit it. And you are easily manipulatable.'

'That's not true.'

'Aaron, do you think it was your choice to drop me? Think about what got me to sit here in the first place.'

'I asked you. You made me ask you?'

'I know how to manipulate you. You are my puppet. And also you cannot multitask.'

He turned back his car, 'No, Des. Imagine this. Do you think about whether aliens exist or not all the time? No, but it will be in your mind always. Just like that, the things happening now occur to occupy the memory. That's normal.'

'Don't bluff. Admit it, Aaron Stitch. Your brain can't multitask.'

'Did you sleep last night?' Karu shattered his thought bubble.

'What?'

'I asked you, did you sleep last night? What happened?'

Did I sleep last night? Yes, I did. What is the matter with my sleep now?

'Can you please stop asking too many questions? I'm having a headache here.' He motioned like his head was going to blast.

She peeped at his hair, 'It's all because of your hair. When did you lastly cut your hair?'

'Does your father run a hair salon? What is the matter with you and my hair?' He rubbed his thick well-groomed not so long beard at her.

'Don't speak about my father,' Karu glared at him. The look of someone can burn a city with their eyes.

Karu wants Aaron to be seen neat with a clean shave and short haircut. But now Aaron's hair looked like it hadn't been cut in two months and beard like it has never touched a blade. Aaron has fair skin, straight jaws, a sharp nose, and light brown eyes. He dressed his muscular body in a white V-neck T-shirt and navy blue jeans.

'What? I like to be in this look. Everyone appreciates me looking good in this way. This brings me confidence in myself. And even Destiny said she likes me to look with a beard.'

Did I say that?

Karu looked suspicious, 'Who's Destiny?'

'Who?'

'You said someone called Destiny likes you with a beard,' her whole face turned the heat on. 'Who?'

'Oh,' he cleared his throat. 'It's just one of my office mates. Not a big deal. Please stop asking questions.'

'But you haven't told me anything about her. This is the first time I'm hearing this name.'

Karu doesn't have many friends. She never believed that friends can make a permanent portion of her life. Aaron has a few permanent friends who are introduced to Karu. He can easily pick who are the important persons in his life. If he mentioned them to Karu, then they are. But Aaron never mentioned Destiny. Or about Karu to Destiny. He didn't know why, he never mentioned Karu to anyone in his office.

'I'm asking you,' she yelled at him.

He held his head between his hands and screamed, 'That's it! My head is breaking. Shut up!'

'Go and get some sleep. I will make the bed for you,' she yelled and pulled him into the cabin.

That frightened Aaron. He didn't want to be stuck in that forest for the whole night. He needed a break from this. A time to think about what would make Karu get away from this forest. But not asking her straight. *But what shall I do? Where shall I go from here in this forest?*

'No, I need a walk,' he released his head from his hands.

'What?'

'I need to take a walk. Maybe it will make me feel better.'

'Walk here,' she showed him the front garden with broken flower pots.

'No, I need some air. Remember the cliff you showed me there. I want to stand there to have a view of the moon.'

'Why do you want to go there at this time? What made you think to go there suddenly?' she yelled.

Aaron yelled back, 'Do I have to report all the things happening in my mind? I just want to go there. Okay?'

'No, you should not go there. It's dangerous. My dad has said there will be elephants or other animals roaming at night. That's not safe to go now.' She said strictly, 'Don't go now.'

There is a joke Aaron tells his parents, "If someone says it would rain, Karu would be seen with her purple umbrella wherever she goes." It's not her fear. It's anticipation. But for Aaron, she thinks of every negative thing that doesn't have any chance to happen.

'I'm going anyway,' He put on his shoes.

'Listen, I can't be alone here. It will scare me. Don't leave me,' she cried out.

'Then why did you choose this place, Karu? Huh?' he stared at her. Her innocent answerless face. 'If you fear to be in your pleasant family vacation house. Then come with me,' he pulled her arms to the stairs.

'No, it's dangerous. Please come back!' she backed off and shouted at him to get back as if he was standing on fire, 'Please come back here!'

'Look Karu. I need to go there,' He pointed at the direction of the cliff. 'Even if you are not coming, I will go. Just ten minutes. What will happen if you come with me?'

She was not speaking anything and clutching a wooden pillar as if he was pulling her. As if he was forcing her to walk on that fire.

'Fine,' he spread his hands and swirled back, 'I'll go alone.'

Watching Aaron from his back changed her mind. 'Wait, I will come with you!'

—— Chapter Four ——

Karu was walking, both hands were twined to Aaron's arm. The tall trees had covered the moonlight. It was all dark there. Aaron could barely see the way through the small moonlight escaped through leaves in the woods. He led the way. His irises opened wider and he noticed Karu's oceans in her eyes were glaring by the darkness of the forest.

How dark are those?

'Aaron, please let's go back,' she beseeched him continuously.

'Let me please find the way,' Aaron walked in the moon's direction.

'You don't know the way. We will be lost. There can be lost ponds wherever we are walking. We will fall into one,' she whined, holding him tight, 'There is no one in this forest to find us. I haven't said to my family I'm coming here.'

'Shhh! It's not a big jungle. It's just dark. Now, just shut up and walk with me.'

Aaron held his palm straight to find things before him, and touched an owl who was watching these two. It hooted and flew over their heads. Aaron pulled her down.

Karu screamed, grabbing the grass on the ground.

'Karu, Stop this!' He stood up.

'Let's go back, Aaron,' she frightened more and pulled him without any knowledge of which way was the cabin.

He threw off her hands, 'Look if you want to go back. Go by yourself. Or else shut up and follow me.'

'Why are you being so rude Aaron?' She yelled, 'You were never being like this before Karan hit you.'

Karu triggered a traumatic memory in Aaron's mind. They both were 20 when that happened. They both were young and lean; their faces were reflecting puberty and shyness to each other. It was a park filled with teenage couples.

'I have to go. If someone I know sees me, I may get into trouble.' Karu was looking around in fear.

'You are treating me so worse, Karu. You show your classmates to your family. You even invite them to your house. What is wrong with me? Why am I the one who is your secret?'

'Try to understand, Aaron. You are not one of them. You are special to me.'

'I regret being your special one. Like some wrong relationship.' He put his long-haired head down. Karu lifted it with her hand.

He looked at Karu's face, 'Come on, Karu, we both are in college now. I have already shown you to my family, my parents like you, my brother and sister are fond of you. I have to tell them what we did today after I get home.'

His words made her blush, 'What is your point?' The pimples on her face turned rosier than the pink shawl's ends twinned loosely in her hands above the white churidar she wore that day.

'What about your family? When will you tell them about me?' Aaron was sitting closer to her on the park bench where they both usually sit.

'I think it is too soon, Aaron.'

'You mean between us?' asked Aaron.

'No, between us it is never soon,' she blushed again. 'I'm saying that my parents don't want me to have a love marriage. After finishing college, they will look for a groom. So, that will be adequate time to talk about you.'

'Huh, groom searching… So, what kind of groom will your father search for you?'

She smiled, 'In my village, there are some rituals. Those are tough.'

'Karu, I'm a tough guy,' he spread his long thin arms revealed from his green t-shirt with monster graphics.

She laughed with her crooked teeth.

'Why are you laughing? Tell me what to do?' He asked.

Karu said with a smile in the corner of her lips, 'Okay, there will be a stone. You have to lift it. It proves that you are worthy to have me.'

'How big the stone will be?'

'Like this,' she spread her palms as much as they could go away.

'That's not a stone. That is a rock. I will be broken.' He laughed and shook his head. 'I don't need to marry you anymore.'

She laughed and said, 'I was kidding it is one of our traditional methods. Now, my father will look at astrology for you and me. If we get matched well nothing can compromise him more than that.'

'Really? Is it that tough to get married to you?'

'Yes, and it can be easy if you have a twisted moustache. My father likes it.'

She twisted his puberty moustache with her fingers. Those henna-coloured fingers touched his lips. He went to kiss her. He breathed her breath.

'You need to tell your brother and sister what we did today,' she murmured.

He smirked. 'I will censor it.'

They both closed their eyes and moved closer to each other.

'Karu!' A shout shattered them both. It was from Karan, Karu's brother. 'What are you doing?'

They both had a panic attack. Karan behaved violently. He pulled Karu's hand on his way to his motorbike.

Aaron was scared but he had to face that. He hurried before them and blocked their way. 'It is not her fault. It was mine. Please don't hurt her.'

'Move away, kid,' Karan warned him. Aaron dared. They both didn't get a good introduction or a nice first impression. But that meeting made Aaron unforgettable.

He slapped him loudly. Karu broke into tears and screamed, 'Aaron, go away.'

Aaron didn't. He was standing there with the palm prints of Karan on his face and watched Karu is being taken from him. *There were many couples in the park. Why I was the only person to stand embarrassed?*

Karu was right. That incident made an impact on Aaron. In time he got tough physically. He felt traumatic every time he thinks about her family and her culture. Every time he lifted a weight in the gym, he checked whether he got the strength to pick up a rock.

'Don't pull that story now. I don't want you to talk to me about him.' Aaron found a ground reflecting moonlight. He walked in the direction.

Karu followed him, 'Why? This is about family, Aaron. We both may be coming from different sides. But we have to work it out. I love your family. Why are you hating mine?'

'When did I say I hate your family?' Aaron argued back.

'You never said you like them either,' she shook her head.

'Look, your mother doesn't believe me. Your brother hates me and your father is being mean to me. He is not willing to give me any chances.'

'When did you ask for the chance?' she yelled, 'How many times have I asked you to come home and have a talk with him?'

'When did he call me? How should I go to someone's house without an invitation? Your family needs a culture, Karu.'

'We have a culture,' Karu stressed the words.

'Unfortunately, that doesn't count nowadays,' Aaron threw his hands in the air.

'If you think like this we will never get together.'

He stopped walking and turned to her, 'You know what? We will never be going to get together. There is no chance for our families to be united,' he raised his voice, 'If we want to do it, we have to do it in our way.'

'No. I can't marry you without my family,' she strongly refused.

'Then you made your choice, Karu,' Aaron started to walk on the meadows.

Karu was quiet, following him for a while. Her ocean was way too louder than ever. They had come out of the woods and stepped on thick meadows shining on moonlight to a stream before them.

The stream was running water like it was pretending to be a river. It was surrounded by large boulders and rocks around the place. The biggest one was the cliff across the stream Aaron was walking to.

Only the flowing stream and frogs on the boulders around them made noises before Karu spoke. She stopped walking, 'You are right, Aaron. I made my choice.'

Aaron signed and turned at her, 'What do you want now, Karu?'

She spoke with a straight-face. 'Let's go back. Drop me in my home. I don't want to be here anymore.'

'Is that what you want? Sure. But now, let's cross this stream,' He took her hand.

She threw him off, 'I'm not coming.'

He yelled, 'Okay fine, I will go then. You stay here. Can you at least do this for me, Karu? I'm just asking you one thing for me. As my special birthday wish to you. Just stay here. Stay here until I come. Then we can talk about everything.'

Karu knew what he said by "everything." Like she was expecting this to happen, she accepted it and waited for that everything to happen.

Aaron pulled up his pants and dived his foot into the stream. He stepped on sloppy rocks, crossed the stream, and reached the bottom of the cliff.

'Careful!' Karu yelled.

'I'm okay!' The cliff was covered with moss. He climbed on it and reached the top.

'Hey, do you know what day is tomorrow?' Aaron asked when he and Destiny were coming out of her apartment door on Saturday.

'I guess I know,' she smiled, 'It's the blue moon day. The second full moon of the month. I was waiting eagerly for this night for the whole year. Tomorrow, I will capture it with my telescope.'

Aaron nodded at her excitement.

'What?' She asked at Aaron's disappointed face.

'Nothing, I didn't know telescopes can capture pictures.'

'No,' she snorted, 'I will connect the DSLR. Like a lens.' They walked on the steps.

'Got it.' Aaron wanted to remind her it was his birthday the next night. But there was a second thought inside him. *What if she already knows and pretends like she doesn't. Just now I wrote it down and she saw it. Anyway, it's worth a shot to spill some words.* 'It's my_'

'Are you free tomorrow night?' she asked when they reached the car.

'Yes! I'm free,' he opened the door.

'Okay, then I will call you. To remind about it. The moon thing.'

She knows! 'Oh, I will be waiting for your call,' he smiled and got into the car.

Aaron reached the cliff and stared at the moon. The moon in the dark purple sky from there looked beautiful. It was full and bright. His eyes needed time to get to know this brightness. He wondered, *Is Des looking at this same moon from her apartment?*

I wish I could be there with her and look into her telescope. Or I wish Des to be here with me, above this cliff, and name all the stars around me. Even if she isn't here I wish to be standing here all night.

Somewhere deep in his heart, he was looking for Karu. When he turned to her from the cliff, she was wiping her tears, couldn't stop crying. Finally, I made her cry on my birthday.

It's not her fault. She never can be the person I want to be. I don't want her to cry like this all day after marrying me. Maybe her life is not meant to be with me. She could be happy with the person her father shows her. Someone with a twisted-moustache, who can lift rocks. That would make her life peaceful. I need to say this to her. Say that this won't work between us and we have to move on. Maybe, I will tell her when we leave. After I drop her off at her house. I will tell her to forget me and do what makes her parents happy. I hope this is the right thing to do for both of us.

He waved his hands to sign her to wait there. He slowly got down from the cliff. Karu was watching his feet on every step until he reached the ground.

When he landed at the ground level, there glowed something in the sky. Aaron noticed it and came to know it was not a satellite. Finally, a star was falling on his birthday. Now he could make a wish for himself. He stopped moving and closed his eyes. He made a wish, *Karu should not be my girlfriend.*

He opened his eyes. He could see his own eyes gleaming. The star was getting bigger. It roared, tearing off the sky with heavy smoke around it. It was coming towards them. There was no time to realize that this was not a star. But Aaron predicted whatever it was, it was going to fall on the place where Karu was standing. Where he wanted her to stay.

What the fuck!

'Karu! Move back! Karu!' He yelled from across the stream. 'Run!'

Karu turned and looked at the sky. Only this could torch her dark eyes.

'Karu!' Aaron dashed towards the stream as fast as he could. But that all happened in an instant. The falling object touched the ground with an enormous power of plasma energy blasted around it. Everything around there was scattered in the air. He was thrown back from the blast. A flying stone hit his forehead and he fell back across the stream.

— Chapter Five —

'Hey, I'm no expert in making the city's best coffee. But I can make one. You want to come over for a cup?' Destiny asked when Aaron finally got the right lane and dropped in front of her apartment.

Aaron nodded, 'I think, I would.' He got out of the car and locked it.

'Is it okay for me to come inside?' he asked before entering the stairs.

'There is no problem, I live alone here.'

'Yeah, I know that much about you.' he followed her to the stairs.

Destiny lived on the second floor of that three-floor apartment. Her neighbours were mostly retired couples. A couple of old ladies stared at Aaron when he entered her block.

It was a small living room and kitchen, on the right to the door that leads to a bedroom on the left, there was a small balcony where a telescope fitted in a tripod. There was a green hard-plastic dining table and chairs for two people.

On a writing desk, papers were scattered. There was a small stack of theory books on her table and an E-book device.

'Are you reading on this? This won't give you the real feel like paperbacks.'

'Oh, come on. They are just papers bound together. And I don't like to sniff them. It's just dust that you feel nostalgic about.'

'What a cynic speech?' He made her laugh.

Aaron looked at a shelf in the corner with lots of medications on top. And the rest of the shelf has scan reports and medical bills on it.

Aaron noticed them. 'So many medicines.'

'Oh, that's for my brain,' she threw her handbag on the table. 'I have some sleeping issues.'

'You are having a lot of coffee and taking sleeping pills. What happened to you?'

'May be a hit on the head.'

'Come on, I was joking.'

'I wasn't. Ugh!' She sighed and threw herself in a green plastic chair. It creaked a little. 'Sit with me. I was met by an accident.'

He sat on the other chair across the table, 'When?'

'Two years ago. Don't ask me for more details. I don't remember what happened before the accident. Or after that for a while.'

Aaron thought it was a joke, but she seemed to be frustrated. 'Seriously?'

'Yes, I don't remember anything of who I was. I was just born newly as a 23-year-old baby and saw my parents. I know the language, I know mathematics, and I know how to ride a bike. But no other information,' she was frozen in a sad face.

She switched a grin swiftly, 'Then I started everything anew. I learned new stuff, studied journalism, wrote blogs, and bought myself a scooter. Only Damian knows about this. And now, it is you.'

Aaron thought Destiny is not so close to sharing her personals. That's why he didn't share his things too. That includes Karu.

'This is why you never spoke of your past.'

'Duh! How can I tell if I don't know what the hell has happened? I had visitors when I was at the hospital. But I don't know who my friends and enemies are. I don't remember my first period, I don't know if I ever had a love and I don't even know if I'm a virgin or not. ' She groaned. 'Sometimes at night I wake up and try to break my head from inside. I scream to myself like "What kind of Destiny were you?"'

'Hey! Are you okay now?'

'Yes, don't freak out. I forgot why you came. Coffee! I will make a coffee, wait.' She got up and walked to the kitchen. And made an instant coffee.

'And you know? My prediction in astrology got more accurate after this injury.' She handed him a cup of coffee and sat back on the chair.

'Really? Are you an astrologist? Someone who sees if the bride and groom are the perfect match? Is it true?' He sipped the coffee.

'That's not the only job. And it's not astrologist. Astrologer! How dare you ask a question like that?' She put the coffee cup on the table and took a notepad.

'Tell me your birth details. Here write it down.' She handed him the notepad.

Aaron wrote the date, time, and place. Destiny scribbled pages and made calculations for a while. She finished the coffee before he did. She was telling things that had already happened to him. Everything was accurate. She even mentioned the tooth pain he got while he was a teenager. 'You are a good astrologer.'

'Thanks. Are you married?'

He spilled the coffee in shock. 'No!'

'Engaged?' She asked sceptically.

'Now, you are a bad astrologer.'

She giggled. 'But you will soon. It says you will get married by this year and get the love of your life.'

Can she find out about Karu? 'Really?'

'Yes, but it says, you will suffer much this year. Maybe you would get hurt, bleed and so much emotional and physical pain I can see.' She felt disturbed by seeing his astrology for this year. 'It will be a total disaster.'

'That's the marriage part probably.' He finished the coffee.

Destiny giggled. 'It's not a joke, Aaron. Be careful.'

'How are you so sure?'

'It's basic. Your birthdate is 19. Your sign is the sun. You are a lone performer. You are sometimes a little aggressive. But also you are emotional at a deep level. And when you are 26, Saturn comes in line. I tell you he's a badass.'

Aaron found the emotional part odd. 'How do these things work? You predict the future.'

'Do you know what is dowsing?'

He shook his head, 'I guess no. Never heard of that.'

'In my village, someone is hired to find the groundwater's location. They can feel the water from the surface. That's called dowsing. It is like one of the Psychic powers. It passes in their generation.'

She took a pack of cigarettes from her cupboard behind her, pulled one out, and lit it with a lighter. 'Don't mind. This is not regular.'

'Okay.'

She blew out clouds of smoke. 'Like that, my late grandfather was an astrologer. And after my mother, I have this gift.'

'So, that's your secret. Did your grandfather teach you all these?'

'Yes. My bad luck, I don't remember him.' She took both the cups and walked to the sink.

'I'm so sorry for him.' Aaron saw a star-shaped pendant without a chain on her table. She was using it as a paperweight. He stole it before Destiny came back.

'It's okay. I don't feel anything.' She came back to sit on the chair.

'So, is this your first job? Why didn't you try for some astrological journalism?' Aaron took this topic to pretend casual like he didn't steal anything from there.

She shook her head. Aaron asked, 'Then, where were you?'

'That, I was working on a weekly magazine.' She exhaled, 'Then it happened again. Suddenly I forgot what happened for like a month. Everyone seems like a stranger to me. Then I couldn't sustain there. So, I left. Without any announcement.' She chortled.

'That's rude.'

'I know. But I like to vanish like that.' She shrugged, 'And I have a prediction that I'm going to vanish from this company also.'

'Why? Don't do that?'

'At least you would like me to stay there. The other staff hate me.'

'It's nothing like that.'

'Come on, Aaron, I know. It's not their fault. I had built a wall around me all the time. I never let anyone get close to me.' She looked depressed. 'And this is why I don't get close to anyone. You know? I may forget them one day.' Tears flowed from her eyes.

'Hey, what happened? You, okay?'

She nodded, 'I'm sorry, I'm not the person who cries like this. But I feel comfortable with you. That makes me weak.' She put her head down.

'It's okay. You can tell me whatever is bothering you.'

'I never built any walls against you. I couldn't. You are the only friend I ever made, Aaron. In my memory.'

He moved closer to her and lifted her chin, 'Don't worry, I won't let you vanish. Even if you forget me, I'm ready to start everything new. I will show you where you can get the best coffee in the city.' That made her smile.

'Thank you,' she whispered. That calmed her. They both went into silence for a while.

Destiny was curling her hair and giving some signals to Aaron. Then she noticed his mind was overfilled by the thoughts of her prediction. His sufferings before marriage.

You can't really multitask, Aaron. She thought.

When Aaron was standing on the cliff, he held that star-shaped pendant in his hand which was glowing in the moonlight. Before he came down, before he saw something in the sky, before he made a wish, before he was thrown back, before he was hit by a flying stone and passed out.

—— Chapter Six ——

Aaron was paralyzed for eight minutes. In those eight minutes, many strange things that will not happen on earth happened. He was dreaming for a while. He dreamt the memory of how he met Karu, the moments time lapsed when he was sleeping in her lap, the memories of 7 years of love they both shared. He heard various echoes of Karu saying his name. Before Aaron came to consciousness, he thought he was dead, then he thought some part of him had been dead.

He woke up below the clouds of smoke. He got injured on the surface of his forehead. He was bleeding. He pushed the wound with his left palm and sat up with a dizzy head. He couldn't feel the pain. Only one thing came into his mind. *Karu!*

'Karu! Where are you? I'm coming!' He stood on his legs and urged to cross the stream. Between the sloppy rocks, he couldn't move fast. He couldn't spot what had fallen from the sky but it should have been something big. It was all smoky. He couldn't see the other side of the stream. The meadows were burning in fire.

His wet shoes reached the ground. The frogs were scattered; the place was quiet. He stood in the middle of the dust and haze. His heart was holding its beats. He could hardly breathe there. 'Karu! Where are you?'

He coughed and kept screaming her name. Before the haze cleared, he was used to seeing through that. He spotted Karu. He can only see her shadow. It's Karu's shape standing in front of all the smoke and fire like she had come out from them. His heart came to ease and he ran to her.

He grabbed her shoulders. She was looking shocked. 'Karu, are you alright?'

She was panting. Her eyes had a confusion.

He fell on her shoulders and hugged her tightly. 'I'm sorry. This is all my fault. I shouldn't have brought you here,' he checked on her for injuries. She had no scratch on her body. 'Good time! You are not injured.'

He felt her skin is so cold in the middle of the burning. 'You are okay, right? Huh?'

She looked shocked.

He shook her. 'Karu! Say something. Have you been hurt somewhere?'

'No, Aaron. I'm good.' Her words came slowly. She noticed his head bleeding, 'You are bleeding. You need…' she thought deeply, '…treatment.'

'I know,' he wiped the blood on his face, 'But I'm okay.' The haze came to fall on the ground, he couldn't see what had fallen there. 'What the hell has happened here? What has fallen here?'

'Aaron, don't go there,' she rushed to block his way. 'I need to talk to you about something serious.'

'Karu, I won't leave you anymore. I promise you.' He kissed her cold cheek. 'We will get back home soon,' he nodded.

Under the smoke, Aaron spotted someone who had fallen on the ground. It was Karu. She was lying unconscious there.

Karu? He rushed to fall on his knees and grabbed her in his arms. She was not opening her eyes, totally flaked out. And the back of her head was bleeding. He lifted her. Her face was not holding up. Her neck had broken badly. He was scared stiff of seeing blood in his hand.

'Karu! What happened to you? I just saw you there alright.' He turned back to check and Karu was still standing there without a scratch. And she was walking to him. He had another Karu in his hands. He could feel the warmth of her body. *This is Karu.*

'Karu, Karu, wake up now.' He quailed to her.

'She can't hear you.' The cold-skinned Karu told him.

'Who are you?'

'I'm sorry, Aaron. Karu is no more,' she spoke with a pang of guilt.

'What the hell is happening here?' he yelled, 'Who are you?'

She bent her knees before him, 'It was an accident.'

He was frightened and confused. 'Who are you in the first place?'

'I don't belong here. I hope you will get what is happening here. I'm the fallen thing,' she made a nod, 'I'm really sorry, I accidentally crashed on her.'

'What? Why? Why are you looking like her?'

'It's because… I took her shape. I do this to whoever I meet first on visiting a new place.' She looked exactly like Karu. The dress was also the same. 'I know it's weird. But believe me. I took her form. I'm not Karu.'

'Karu, please wake up! We have to leave from here.' He pulled her close to his face. He broke into cries in her ears. 'I'm sorry, I shouldn't have left you alone. Wake up please.'

'She's dead, Aaron.'

'No, she's not,' he screamed.

'I'm sorry, Aaron. And it's not your fault.'

Aaron was shaking, 'Look, whatever you are, you have killed her. You killed the person who I love the most in my life. I'm not going to leave you_'

'But you don't love her,' she shook her head. 'You wished her not to be yours. "Karu shouldn't be my girlfriend."'

'Yes, I did. But that doesn't mean I want her to be dead.' He cried out like never before. His tears were falling on Karu in his hands. 'I love her. I truly love her.'

'You did. But now, you can only think of the girl named Destiny.'

'It's not true!' he screamed his refusal. 'What I said from there to you is not true. And I know that I love Karu. Okay? And I will save her on whatever it takes.'

'Her neck is broken, don't make it more complicated, Aaron,' she yelled.

He didn't listen to her. He grabbed Karu and lifted her. He supported her neck in his palm. 'Karu! What have I caused you?' he pulled her tight and cried on her face. 'I love you. I love you, Karu.'

Karu in her hands started to stir. She coughed twice. Her eyes remained close. Her heart functioned. She was still unconscious.

'Karu, Karu, are you okay, Karu! Look at me. Karu....' he held her neck and tried to wake her up. 'She is alive. She is alive!'

'Yes, she is!' Another Karu was surprised.

'I need to get to my car. Where is my car?' he looked around to know where they were.

'No, wait, bring her here,' she pointed to a massive boulder beside the stream. Aaron had no idea of what was the purpose of that.

She went to the boulder and tapped on it. A part of it opened like a door. Aaron could only see the light source fell on the ground from the doorway.

'Take her inside. Quick,' she came to pick Karu from him.

He shook his head, 'Why should I? I need to get her to the hospital.'

She tried to pull Karu from Aaron. He shouted, 'You go away! Don't touch her.'

'Bring her here, Aaron. I can save her life. This is the only way. Believe me. You have no choice. You can't make it to the hospital. Look where we are now.'

Aaron looked around and stumbled in confusion. He stood still but was about to faint. Her screaming echoed in his head, 'We are losing her, Aaron. Bring her. Hold her neck tight.'

There was nothing here a few minutes before. Where did this rock come from? Was this the falling object? An asteroid? Is this an alien?

'Are you listening? Bring her here. She needs to breathe!'

Aaron came back to attention. He ignored his confusions. The only thing he wanted was to save Karu. He picked Karu up and followed the mysterious person.

— **Chapter Seven** —

Life isn't normal if you make a wish to a star and then the star fell on your girlfriend's head. I'm listening to an alien. This is the weirdest thing I did in my whole life. Maybe this all could be a dream. A nightmare. I'm still 25 now. I love Karu. Only Karu is in my mind. Wake up! Wake up, idiot! Don't listen to it. Wake up!

Sadly, it was not a dream. Aaron entered the door with Karu in his arms. He supported her broken neck in his palm. The room was warm. He looked around. The cubicle had one part like a cave with roots mushroomed on the wall. The other side of the cave had most of the white floor built on it.

'Come over,' she went to a machine that looked like a bed but a capsule with glass closure. She opened and thick white fog released from it like a freezer. 'Drop her into this.'

'What is this?' Aaron was freaked out.

'It will put her in hibernation. Then analyse the injuries and fix her tissues.'

It looked like a tomb. But more like a machine. A memory of Karu holding him tight in the fear of standing on a mall escalator until they reach the floor flashed in Aaron's mind. Aaron was embarrassed by her that day.

'No, I'm not putting her into this.' he backed off.

'Aaron, you have to trust me. It will heal her. Listen, we don't have time for this.'

'Tell me, why do you want to help us?'

'Because it was all my fault,' she yelled, 'I don't want anyone to die in front of my eyes.' She looked at his faint eyes and said, 'You know Karu will do this if it is her in my place.'

Like it was his cornerstone, Aaron dropped Karu in that bed and stepped back. She closed the glass. A yellow light projected over Karu. Soon, a cloud of frost surrounded her.

'What is happening?'

'She will be alright. Believe me, it will make her heal as soon as possible.'

It's all fiction. The thing standing before me. The thing I'm inside. The thing I put Karu in. It's all so fiction that I never heard of. I'm so tired. If this is a dream, I'm not going to sleep anymore for the rest of my life.

He was sweating. He studied the things around him. In front of him across Karu, the cave wall stood empty. On his right, a table and three white stools with black cushions in a cylindrical shape were levitating a foot from the ground. He pointed one of them to her.

'It's okay. Have a seat. Relax please.'

He pulled the stool. It was projecting a blue light to the floor. He sat on it with a baffled face. It was weird for both of them. 'Who are you?'

'You can call me Cara.'

'You have a name?'

'Who hasn't?' She tied her arms.

'First of all, can you turn into something else? Don't be like Karu. It's awkward to me. Please change yourselves.'

'I can't,' she shrugged.

'What does it mean that you can't? You can. Or else how can you be… looking like her?'

'It needs a lot of energy, Aaron. Didn't you see how tired I was when you first saw me? I have to tear off all my molecules and chain them together. It will take more time to regain all my energy. Until then I will be like this,' she spread her arms.

'What?' he squinted, 'What is this place? Where does this come from?'

Cara said, 'It is a starship, used to travel through space. In the place I come from, we are genetically advanced in…' she was thinking like she has a dictionary in her mind, 'Bio-science, to say in your language. You understand?'

'Clearly no.'

'We have these abilities inherited. We can shift our shapes and merge into our surroundings. Currently, this starship has camouflaged itself.'

He looked around for any signs of starships he had ever imagined. There was a table with a plate of sliced roots, water in a fancy jug. He noticed a glass tank, in it a couple of fishes with only cornea as their body swimming in green water. There was something else green in it hiding from him. Nothing matched his imagination. 'How do you drive this?'

'Oh, that's not me. Every ship will have a living being to control. Mine is called Phrix.' Phrix? She searched around, 'Phrix, where are you?'

Aaron looked around. There was no sign of any species around him other than a Karu-shaped alien.

'Phrix, come out. It's safe now. Phrix!'

'What if it has gone outside_' Aaron jerked when his stool quaked. He held it tight and was frozen for a second.

Then he fell from the stool when it moved and escaped from him. It whistled.

'Phrix! What happened to you?' She followed the stool.

He sat up and saw her speaking to the stool. It went fast, whistling, and hit on the corner of the room. It stumbled. He screamed, 'What is that?'

'That's Phrix.' Cara bent her knees down to it. 'Phrix, listen. There is nothing dangerous here. No one will harm you. Everything has come back to normal. Look at me.'

The stool rotated to her like it had a face. It made some weird noises. Like a baby bird.

'Are you okay?' she clasped the stool. It chirped. 'Good! Come with me.' she stood and patted on it.

Aaron looked at her coming to him. The stool was following her. 'What is that creature still doing under the stool?'

She chuckled and lifted the stool. The light from the bottom hit on his face, 'Look, there is nothing under it. Phrix was so scared in the crash, so it changed its form into a stool.'

'A stool?'

'Yes, I told you. It is a camouflage,' she dropped it down. It ran with shame to hide behind her.

'What camouflage? How is this all possible?' he stood up yelling at her.

'Possible what?'

'This ship! You! You look like Karu, this machine, this stool, and everything here. It's all new to me,' he crushed his head with his arms.

'Well, the universe is expanding and it is not your fault, you all are just rotating in the same place over billion years.'

'So, your people are more developed. Evolved. How long have you travelled to reach this unevolved planet? And why did you come here? To mess up my life?'

'How long? The entropy will blow your head. And I'm a lost explorer.' She noticed his bleeding forehead, 'You have been hurt. Haven't you?'

'No, I'm okay.' He hid his wound in his hand, 'Just I got hit by a stone when you almost killed my girlfriend.'

'I don't think you are okay. Come here,' she moved to him.

He backed off and warned her, 'Please leave me.'

Cara dipped her hand into the fish tank and took out something alive and green with tentacles crawling. She stuck it on his wound.

'What are you doing? Ahh! It burns my head,' he jerked, screaming, 'What the fuck are you doing?'

She didn't like him yelling at her like that. Karu's emotions were growing inside her but not her rights. She took off the green thing, 'There you go. Good now?'

'That was painful!' he grunted.

'Huh, you will not survive if you leave your atmosphere,' she shook her head like disappointed by the human race.

'I know that,' he shrieked, checking his wound. It disappeared. 'What have you done? What is that?' he asked about the green creature.

She squinted, 'Wound-Eater? To say in your language?'

'Will Karu be healed like this?' He wiped the moisture on his head.

'I hope so,' she nodded and dropped the wound-eater back in its tank.

'Whatever… Will it hurt Karu like this?'

'No, it's a different kind of process. No pain but it will take some time.'

He looked at Karu. She was sleeping as nothing had happened. *Stay there, Karu. We will go home soon.*

He looked at his watch and realised it was malfunctioning. He removed it and placed it on the table. He checked the time on his phone. It was 2.30 in the morning. *Oh, shit. What will I say to Karu's parents? And to my parents?*

'How long will this take?' he asked in an urge to go.

'Perhaps… 120 hours.'

'What?' he shouted, 'It's like… Five days?'

'Yes. Five days. It's not magic. Okay?'

'Listen I can't freak out Karu's parents by showing you and all of your alien things,' she was triggered when he said alien. She stared at him. But those eyes had no heat like Karu's. He ignored it easily. 'I need to admit her to a hospital right now. I'm calling for an emergency.'

'No! You shouldn't,' she shouted.

Aaron took out the phone again. 'Oh! Crap! There is no phone signal! Why did you bring me here in the first place, Karu?'

Cara screeched at him. 'Please don't make any calls. And please you shouldn't tell anyone about what happened here?'

'Why is that?'

'Because as you said it will freak out everyone. I don't want to be stuck on this planet of yours. I have some rules. I need to get back to my place secretly from here. That's good for everyone. Believe me. I'm asking you this as a help.'

'Why? Why should I help you? Tell me a reason.'

'You should. Because I have your girlfriend,' she gestured at Karu.

'Are you threatening me?' he stared at her.

'No, I'm not. I'm helping you. To heal her. See.'

He shouted out, 'For god's sake, you caused this to her!'

'Okay fine,' Cara closed her, took a deep breath, and opened her eyes, 'Let's make a deal.'

Aaron was staring at her, waiting for her to speak.

'You should keep my secret. And I will be your girlfriend until she gets healed.'

'What? I'm sorry I can't understand what the hell are you saying? How can you… possibly be my girlfriend?' he rumbled, 'You cannot. Because my girlfriend is here, trapped in your hell. And she will be trapped for five more days.'

'Look at me, idiot,' she spread her hands, 'I'm in front of you as the girl who you want. I can pretend to be her in front of her family.'

'You can't be Karu because you look like her. If they know, her brother will kill me,' Aaron shook his head with a fake grin.

'I know what happens between you and her brother.' she threw a piece of information, 'He hit you hard once you were a teenager. Karu thinks it has changed you from a romantic charming person to this kind of arrogant.'

'That's not true,' Aaron tied his arms and felt suspicious about this.

'Yes, it is. How toxic were you to her?'

'Wait, how do you know all this? You said my name when I saw you there for the first_' He stopped speaking.

'Say it!' she nodded once.

'You read my mind?' he pointed at her.

'Yes, I read you and also her. Now I have her memories. I don't have them all. But trust me, I can take relevant events by merely touching people. Whoever I touch, I get access to their memories and I would act like knowing them.'

'No, the world out there is not a game. I don't know what you will be turned into. I don't want to risk everyone in this.'

'You have to believe me, Aaron. This is the only choice we have right now. I swear; no one will get harmed. And I will return after she gets healed. I promise you,' she pledged. 'Think about it.'

Aaron turned to Karu. He looked at her in a silent state. Her oceans were fully calm. He didn't have any idea when he could see those eyes again.

I caused her this situation. I should not have brought her to the stream. I shouldn't have left her alone. I should not have made that wish. It was all my fault. And now I don't know if I have any other way to undo all these.

Aaron took the covenant.

— Chapter Eight —

Things were quite different when Aaron was driving back home. He felt the distance between him and Karu was growing when his wheels moved. A Karu was sitting beside him in the passenger seat. But she couldn't cheat his heart as she could do to his eyes. He was worrying about Karu. He kept asking Cara questions. *Will she breathe comfort there? Will anyone come there? What if the stool takes off from there?*

Cara answered him without getting frustrated. She had no emotions but she respected his concern for Karu. Aaron asked a few more questions and went back to silence.

After they came out of the boulder, Aaron blew off the fire on the meadows whilst Cara spoke to Phrix. She warned it. 'Phrix, you should stay here until I come back. You should not open or give any signals unless I call you. You should respond only to me. Understand?'

It mourned chirps. She rubbed its seat on the head. 'Don't be scared. I will be back soon. Take care of her.' She closed the doorway. It turned into a normal rock surface without any signs. They left the cabin as it was and hit the car on the road.

They reached Elysian City when Karu's mobile on the car deck rang. The display threatened Aaron with a name.

He slammed the steering, 'Oh, Crap! It's Karu's brother.'

'I'll talk,' Cara hurried to pick the phone.

Aaron grabbed it. 'No, they might have already found out that I and Karu were together. I have to face it.'

Blink 'Hello?'

'Who is speaking? Where is Karu?' Karan from the other end asked in doubt.

'It's Aaron speaking. Karu is with me.'

'What?' he sounded staggered.

'Yes, she is with me now. Today's my birthday and she wanted to spend some time in our house. Look, we didn't have a phone signal over there,' he tried to explain.

'She told us that she was going to her friend's birthday party. I knew there must be something wrong. That's why I called to check,' he said over the phone.

Crap! They don't know. I messed up.

'Well, as I said, it's my birthday. We celebrated with my family. What's wrong_' He turned to Cara who was curious about their conversation, 'Okay, fine. Wait for 15 minutes. I'll drop her at your house.'

'Are you coming here?'

'Yes, I'm on my way.'

'Dare yourself to come here, kid. Hope you won't go back normally.'

Aaron changed the gear. The engine roared under his foot. 'Oh yeah, what do you think you are?' He yelled at him on the phone, 'Let's see that. I'll be there faster than I said.' He hung up.

'Aaron, you okay?' She felt his anger and some other strong trauma than she expected. 'You need to calm down.'

'Please don't say anything,' he accelerated the engine.

'What happened?'

'It's not your worry.'

'Yes, it is. We made a deal.'

He sighed, 'Karu's parents. They know where we are. And they are waiting for us to show up.'

'What did he say? Why do you look so much in anger?'

'Can you please keep quiet for a while?' He went back to his silence but drove fast, tightening his teeth.

She moved her hand towards him and touched his shoulder. He stared at her face, his Karu's face. She gasped.

'What?' He asked.

'Did you fight back with her brother?'

Yes, I fought back. I don't want to go into details. After college, it happened again. He tried to take Karu away from me, again. But I didn't leave her. He slapped me again. I hit him back hard. Harder than I anticipated. The two years of rage answered on his face. I felt so heroic on that day. But the consequences didn't end well. Karu was broken between me and her family. Those are the moments I want to forget but still floating up when I think about her family. Why Karu? Why is it hard to get close to your family? And why do I have to? I still don't know.

He drove into Karu's street and pulled over his car at the gate. The lights in her house were still on. No one had slept. *This means they all are waiting for us to arrive.*

'Listen_' Aaron started.

'Don't worry about anything. I will take care of everything from here,' Cara jumped from her seat. 'Don't speak to her brother. It's not good for now. It is better you leave me from here.'

He took a breath, 'First of all, don't read my memory. I'm warning you,' he looked sharply at her face, 'Will you?'

She shrugged. 'Okay fine. I won't.'

'That's good.' He pocketed his mobile phone. And handed Karu's phone to her. 'Keep this. Text me through this application_'

'Yes! I know.'

He stared at her. 'Do you have any other special powers?'

'Yes, I'm a terrific actor. I can pretend to be anyone I want.'

'It's called talent. Not a power. Let's get off now,' he opened the car door, 'Come with me.'

They came out and walked to the house. Aaron had come to this house many times. But not as invited, he had sneak-peeked to meet Karu. Whenever her parents were out to other towns or for a long shopping trip, Karu would be alone and call Aaron. He would come and they had spent their most lone-times in her room. After what happened with Karan in the park, Aaron felt ashamed of sneak-peeking. That was the reason why he refused to come to the house. The reason why he dropped Karu at the street corner every time.

'Do you know what time is this?' Karan's voice unwelcomed him before he entered the porch. He blocked the doorway and yelled at this innocent alien.

Cara had no idea what was happening. Her eyes met Aaron for an answer.

'That's him. Karu's brother,' Aaron whispered.

'It's all because of you.' he walked furiously to Aaron. And Aaron didn't move. He held his breath and stared at him. They both tightened their fists.

'Wait…' Cara came between them and held Karan's arms, 'Wait, Karan. It's not his fault. Don't get angry. Listen to me, I told you, I'm going to a birthday party with my friends. What is wrong if it is his birthday?'

'You lied to me,' he raised his hand to slap her.

Aaron pulled her to his side, 'Don't dare to touch her.'

Karan busted into anger, 'I'm her brother.'

'So what? Didn't your parents teach you not to raise your hand on a woman?' Aaron tried to roast him more, 'Raise on me if you have the guts.'

'Stop it! Stop whatever you two are doing there.' Karu's father shouted standing in front of the door. They both released their fists out of respect.

'Karan, go to your room. I will look after them.'

He yelled, 'There is nothing to look after. Let's finish everything here.'

'I told you to go now,' his father ordered. Karan left the place with a fixing stare on Aaron. Aaron stared back until he disappeared into the house.

'Bring him inside,' he told Cara and turned to walk inside.

Cara asked Aaron, 'Who was that?'

Aaron put his head down. 'Might be your father, I think.'

'Oh! Okay. I got it. I will take charge from here.'

'Did he say that? Karu's father?'

'Yes, I went inside and sat on the sofa he insisted. He told Karu to go to her room. Then her mother was scolding me on one side, his brother was smashing things in his room then all of sudden, him, Karu's father he just said, "In our family there are traditions. We won't let our girl go out before marriage. Importantly in nights. I hope you understand that." Then I apologized and told him it was my birthday.'

'That was when he said, "Let's make an engagement. You and Karu with you. It will be held in this house as our family tradition. Will you and your family be okay with that?" He asked this. I was surprised. Her mother was dumbstruck. The breaking noises stopped from that room.'

And that alien. I realized what it told me that acting is one of its powers. After getting into the house, it turned into the real Karu. Karu's mother was shouting at it. It reacted like it was guilty. I was never freaked out like that before. It used Karu's memories. What Destiny said about psychic powers is true. I got relaxed only after it went on the stairs to Karu's room.

'And you said yes?' Aaron's mother asked while his whole family was interrogating him what happened at Karu's home. Aaron maintained the same lie between both families.

He spread his hands, 'What else I can say? This is the first time he is speaking to me. This man has asked me for something. I need to do something responsible for him. So, I said yes.'

His father said, 'I think that is a good idea. Anyway, Karu is coming to our home as your wife someday. Isn't it?' Everyone else nodded at him. 'And it's the correct time for the engagement. So, Aaron, I will give you your grandmother's ring. All you have to do is just ask her.'

'No, dad. They are planning a pre-wedding ceremony in their house. Like a proper engagement with rituals and family guests. He told me to invite our relatives and guests too.'

'How will it be? This traditional engagement.' His mother asked.

'I know!' Stella exclaimed, 'My friend's sister had an engagement like that. I went there. Remember mom?'

'Yes, Stella. Speak up.'

'They will exchange rings in front of all and they would announce the wedding date there.'

'Exchanging rings? That's called marriage.' Aaron's father was alarmed.

'No, dad. In marriage, the groom will tie up a pendant in the bride's neck.' Stella explained.

'I remember our neighbour… who is that… they moved from the south?' His mother asked Mr. Stitch.

'Nah… They are nuts.' He replied, 'They didn't even invite us.'

'Dad! Mom! Everyone!' Aaron interrupted them. 'I'm doing this just for her parents. Okay? There is no big deal. We just need to go there and be a part of the ceremony. Invite only our close relations.'

'When is the engagement?' Mrs. Stitch asked.

'Tomorrow. It seems like they have some trouble with their relatives, because of this, I and Karu. I mean, they have come up for us this much. So, we should be with them now.'

His mother exhaled. 'Huh… Alright. Whatever, we have to do for Karu. I couldn't get a better daughter-in-law than her.'

'Yes! For Karu,' Stella got excited. 'We have to go shopping. To buy the ring and clothes for all of us.'

'Yes! Then, can we get a day off from school today?' Edward asked.

'Calm down, children. Let me think,' Mrs. Stitch was thinking so deeply. 'Okay, I will speak to the class teacher. And we all can go shopping. We have to buy something for them as it is the first time we are going to their house.'

'You guys deal with that.' Aaron walked to his room, 'I'm going to sleep. I have to go to the office in the morning.'

'Wait, we all are still awake, waiting for you.' Stella called him back.

'For what?' he asked.

'Let's cut the cake!' Edward rushed to open the fridge.

'No, I'm so tired. Let's do that in the morning.' Aaron waved his hand and entered his room. He looked at the disappointed family but shut the door. Uff!

They all were knocking for a while and gave up.

—— Chapter Nine ——

The moonlight fell on the floor through the doorway of the dark room. It was bathing her, Clem was sitting on the floor embracing her knees. The scene was like a realistic deception and she was there like a piece in a painting.

She felt a vast emptiness in her mind. However, she tried to dig up the things buried in her mind, nothing was coming up. Her mind was warning her about the ghosts imprisoned in the depths. The vagueness filled the upper most part which was pretentious to what happened.

Something must have happened, she thought, something should be still there under this immense elusiveness.

Clem had never thought of death. That night she was just about to fall into the pit of the grim and somehow coped to survive. She was falling from the height. Her heartbeats were racing. She was scared it would stop beating. Her mind ran a marathon of memories.

She was finally on the ground. All over her body ached, including her eyes from the pain of closing them tightly. She let it go and opened her eyes. She discovered what death tastes like. It was like ashes in her throat that smelled of suffocation.

Her mind was blank. Everything seemed disbelieving for her. It all happened in one night and that is because of the person who she believed. When she found that life was at the edge, she decided to overpower everything she desired. She decided to continue her mission.

Cara snooped out of Karu's room when she heard an early morning television show. She came down and checked the living room. No one was watching the television. It was just background noise. Karu's father in a white cane and tube sarong was reading the newspaper quietly on the wooden sofa with cushions arranged on it.

'Did you brush your teeth?' Karu's mother in her nightdress asked her.

What's brushing? 'Mmm? Yes.' She grinned.

'Come and eat,' she ushered Cara to sit on the chair of the dining table where Karan was eating. He had dressed ready to go to his engineer job.

'You should be so lucky. Your father spoke to your guy last night. We are fixing an engagement. You might have heard it from him, I know. I'm telling you. You should be glad that your father is taking a big risk in this. Understand?'

She nodded and the mother placed three *idlie*s on her plate, 'What is this?'

'Oh!' You forgot what *idli* is?' Karan asked. 'Maa! Give her toast and orange juice. She's the one from that Stitch family now. She forgot how to eat with hands.'

'Keep quiet and eat, Karan.' His mother said and filled his bowl with *sambhar*.

'See this, madam. I will demonstrate it to you. You have to take a piece and dip it in the sambhar. And then put it into your mouth.' He did as he said.

Cara didn't get his sarcasm. She tried it and said, 'It's very delicious. Thank you!'

'Maa! She is making me angrier!' he shouted.

Cara took over all three *idlies*. It almost choked her throat. The mother quickly patted on her head and gave her water, 'Eat slowly, girl,' she turned to Karan, 'Stop scolding her! You made her choke. We don't know how long she will be in this house.'

Cara read her mind for memories in those pats. She felt a mixed emotion that she had never seen from anyone. The mother felt happily satisfied and also a part of her was still sad. She asked Cara, 'You want more Idlies?'

'No, Maa, I'm enough,' she replied.

'Wash your hands and speak to your father.'

She washed her hands in tap water and walked to Karu's father. She sat beside him. She didn't know what to say or how to start a conversation. She held his forearm for memories. That stopped him from reading the newspaper and he looked back at her.

When Karu was a little girl, he used to drive her to school on his scooter. Karu stood between him and the handlebar. She enjoyed pressing the horn button much. She kept pressing it even at unnecessary times. To avoid that he put his thumb behind that rectangular button and halted it from functioning. When Karu tried to push the button, it hurt him a little, still, he hid it and said it was repaired. Little Karu believed it.

He couldn't cheat Karu like that anymore. She had grown up. She had asked for Aaron. He had to give her the life that she wished for. For that, he had to face embarrassment from his relatives in his village. He feared people who would judge him for making this decision. Still, he preferred his daughter's wish to his pride.

He was upset when Karu said she wanted to marry Aaron. He was distraught when Aaron and Karan fought. But last night, when Aaron stepped in his house, something had altered in him. When he saw Aaron defending Karu from her brother bravely, it appeared to him naturally that Aaron is the one.

There was only one way to solve all these problems. This engagement. Nothing can stop when the wedding date is announced. Terminating a wedding would be considered a bigger humiliation than he already had. This sudden engagement was his only plan. Still, he was in the guilt of a promise he made a long time ago.

'Karu?' he broke the connection with Cara, 'What happened?'

Cara felt so emotional. She was never cared this much by anyone; in all the places she had visited so far in the universe. For the first she felt tears in her eyes. She lived her whole life with just ethics. Not emotions. The first emotion she felt was the guilt of what she did to Karu. Now she felt many emotions in this house. She hugged him. 'Thank you, father.'

He wrapped his arms around her and patted on her hair. He was not so open to his daughter. 'Get ready soon. We are going shopping. We have to buy jewels and dresses for tomorrow. I have to speak to the catering people. You go now.'

Cara got up and moved to her mother, 'Maa! Thank you, Maa,' She hugged her. She felt the highest level of love in the universe. A friendly companionship that kept her to hug a little longer.

The mother cracked her knuckles around her face (Karu's face) and kissed her forehead, 'Go and get ready, Karu.'

Cara left her and turned to Karan who was still eating. 'Brother!'

'Stay away from me!' He warned her, 'Your drama won't work on me.'

His mother moved to her husband and said, 'I have never seen her this happy.'

Cara hugged his head from the back while he was sitting, 'Thank you, Brother.'

'I have not accepted this wedding.'

She read him. He has a lot of love and care, a fond on his little sister inside him covered by a wall of ego. She felt secure in this hug.

'I know you will, Thank you.'

'Look at her,' the mother says again, 'How happy she is.'

'I know,' The father replied, 'This marriage.'

Karan got out of her arms and asked, 'Are you taking drugs?'

Meanwhile, Aaron was stirring in his bed. His muscles were painful because of the fall. He didn't sleep a drop that night. He was thinking about Karu all the time. He cried. Like a gate was opened, he couldn't close it again. It *was all my fault.*

He waited for the alarm to go off. Before that, the phone beeped with text messages. Some programmed logarithm built by his company has posted a photo of Aaron in a birthday wish E-card. As he expected, the group messages were filled with wishes including Nazir's. Damian sent a voicemail, wishing him a private message. But there were no messages or calls from Destiny.

On hearing those beeps, the family gathered again before the door. Stella hooted, 'Aaron, I know you are awake. Come out! You can't escape now.'

Aaron remained calm.

'Aaron, the cake is melting, please open the door. We are hungry,' Edward mourned.

'He is scared of candles, I think,' his dad sounded cheerful, 'Or! Or! We can tell him to blow the candle from the keyhole. We can take the rest of the work.'

Stella said, 'Great idea! I will cut the cake on the behalf of my brother.'

'Aaron!' his mother knocked.

'Why should you cut the cake? I'm his brother too.' Edward argued.

'Yeah, but I'm his favourite. Not you!'

'That's not true!'

'Shut up, children,' his mother knocked again, 'Aaron, are you tired now?'

It's not that I'm tired or that I'm remembering the last year. I can't do this celebration when Karu is injured and locked up there. I don't even know how to make a fake smile. I don't know how I'm going to make this engagement happen with some alien in the form of Karu. All I know is it is not my Karuvizhi.

It is not my girlfriend.

—— Chapter Ten ——

Three years before, all Aaron was interested in were cars, motors, and engines. After Aaron assaulted Karan, Karu's parents house-prisoned her. That was his time of despair.

Six weeks after that, he got a chance to speak to her on the phone. He was dying of missing her. But Karu sounded calm and mature.

'Don't be scared, Karu. You just walk in to my home. My parents won't say anything. We can deal with your parents later.' He said in the phone call.

'Aaron, you don't understand the situation I'm in right now. I don't want to choose either you or my family. I can't come like that, Aaron.'

'What the hell are you talking, Karu? What about us?'

'Aaron, I need to talk about you to my father. But I can't talk to him now. You are jobless. I know you have just graduated. But what shall I introduce you to him as? You need to get a career first. I should say something about you proudly. Until then I can't come to your house. Please focus on what you need to do in your career.' She hung up. After five minutes Aaron received a text message from her.

– Aaron, my father came. I will call you when I get the chance again. Remember what I said. I love you. DO NOT REPLY.

That made Aaron pursue his post-graduation in Business Administration. He didn't want to risk his time on some business. He was so clear to get a job. Luckily, he got an internship in SYS and the muse of Karu's words made him work hard. He did all this for Karu. Which made him get a job, become the creative head, and buy a car in which he could sit in his reserved parking area. But where did he lose that purpose? When did he lose that muse? He asked himself.

Aaron got out of the car and walked to the sixteen-floored glass and metal wall building. He wore a grey shirt tucked in light brown pants. He wore his office shoes and a sling bag on his shoulder. He reached the corridor and waited for the elevator to open.

Anyone could say he was thinking deep on seeing his face. It had happened before. He came to this building for the first time with this same confused nervous face. Aaron didn't know he would be this important in this company. That day in this elevator he met a man who encouraged him. That was Damian. He gave him his cheerful good luck wishes. That gave Aaron confidence to lose his self-doubt. He never again thought low of himself.

He was thinking of what happened last night. *What have I done? Some alien in Karu's place in her home. I have set a serpent in their house. This is a risk to her family. I don't feel good about this. I sense something wrong is happening about this alien.*

A sudden flashlight disturbed his thoughts and his restless eyes. Nazir clicked a bizarre photo of Aaron. He cackled, 'Happy birthday, boy! Aaron!'

Aaron cleared his throat that hasn't spoken to anyone for a long time. 'Thank you, sir.'

'You look tired. Are you okay?'

'I'm good.'

'Huh… Then I will catch you at the meeting.' Nazir walked out for his morning break.

Oh! The meeting! That is today? Aaron was about to make a presentation about his new research on a client project.

He went into the elevator. His phone beeped. Nazir had uploaded the photo to the group. There were no messages from Destiny. He tried to call her.

Her phone was switched off.

When you work in a media or advertising space you can come to know all the information before common people. Importantly, gossips. Gossips about all the celebrities in the city will be the main talk of the workplace. Like who owns what? Who loves whom? Who adjusted for whom?

SYS was no exception to that. Aaron and Destiny are not involved in a department that has gossips. But they both were the hot couple who were gossiped about. Everyone kept saying they both were in love. Some asked directly. Some just gossiped around. They both knew it and had discussed it only once in this elevator.

'Hey, yesterday, Sprayman asked me if we both are in a relationship,' Destiny asked Aaron four months ago, when they both were in the elevator. 'Like… "Is Aaron your best friend or boyfriend?"'

'Maybe Sprayman is interested in you.' Aaron pressed the 12th and 15th-floor buttons.

'No, but Mr. Shrugs asked me once too. Is that causing you any problem?'

He shook his head. 'No, but this explains to me why Dark chocolate smiles at me for no reason. She sometimes notices us talking like she has never seen me talking.'

'Hmm…Is that the way we behave?'

'I don't think so… Nazir once teased me with this too.'

She sighed, 'Ugh! What is the matter with these elder people involving in our relationships? Can we go to them and ask them "Looks like you both are having a secret affair, huh? Do both of your spouses know this?" Can we, Aaron?'

Aaron chortled, 'They all just think what they had done in our age. It is not our fault. Do you have any problem with that?'

'Nope. I think it all started from Robot-pants. I know it would be him,' Destiny told him doubtfully.

'Huh… then we should rename him to Rumour-pants.' Aaron stepped out of the elevator to the 12th floor. 'See you in the evening!'

She giggled. 'See you, Major.'

As Aaron entered the 12th floor, the Sprayman, Josh wished him first. 'Happy birthday, Aaron.'

Everyone else in the office was waiting for his arrival since they had seen Nazir's post. They all walked out from their cabins and shook hands with him.

Aaron was a little embarrassed. He forced himself to smile and thanked them back. He tried to brush off everyone and hurried to his cabin. Through the blurry glass door, he saw someone sitting on his chair.

He opened the door and found the so-called dark chocolate, Nancy from the Human Resource sitting before his computer. 'Nancy? What are you doing here?'

She gasped on seeing him. 'Hey, Aaron. You almost scared me.' She faked her panting, 'I was waiting for you.'

'Why? For what? And what are you doing on my PC?' He found it turned on.

'Nothing, it was on when I came here. And I came here to decorate. See.' She pointed him the glittering rice lights, saying "Happy Birthday". 'How's it?'

'Very nice. Thank you. I have some work. Can you please go to your place? I want to be alone for a while.'

'Yeah sure. Sorry for disturbing you.' She walked out of his room, 'Hey! Happy birthday!'

'Thank you,' Aaron closed the door.

He sank into his chair and checked into his phone. He had received messages from Karu's number. But it was not Karu. They were from Cara. She had sent him some photos of engagement dresses and a caption below that.

– Hey, Aaron. Look at the sarees. Which should I choose? Select one for Karu.

The dresses were folded. He couldn't see what types of clothes were those. He just noticed colours. Aaron replied.

- Purple one

She likes Purple.

And she had sent him some group photos of her with Karu's family in the clothing store, in a jewellery store, in a restaurant, and in an Ice-cream bar. *Fine, this alien has started to live Karu's life.*

He kept off his phone aside and poured himself into work for two hours. He couldn't concentrate on his quality checks of the advertisement designs that had to send to the newspaper agency for that week. He approved everything without even looking at them. And a few minutes later, he applied for leave for a week.

Then a call from Damian arrived, 'Hey Aaron. The meeting has started. Are you coming?'

'Yes, Sir. I'm on my way.'

Aaron rushed to the 15th floor in the elevator. He crossed Destiny's cabin. But he found her chair was empty and the desktop was turned off. He walked to her cabin and asked her co-worker, a senior-aged man. 'Ahh… Hi, Sir. Do you know where Destiny is?'

He just shrugged to Aaron, 'She hasn't come to the office, I think. Did you try to call her?'

'Oh, I tried. It is switched off.'

He shrugged again, 'Well, son, if you want some company to drink a coffee, I can come. What do you say?' He cackled at Aaron.

'Thank you, Sir. But I have to catch a meeting. Let's take a rain check.'

'I know you won't come with me.' He murmured and shrugged for the third time. Aaron ignored him and rushed to the meeting.

Aaron reached the conference room. The conversation had started already. He made a quick scan of the room. Destiny was not there.

Damian paused his speech when he opened the door, 'Get inside, Aaron.'

'Hello, everyone. Hi, Sir,' he nodded at some foreign ambassadors for whom he had prepared the presentation.

'This young man is Aaron Stitch, our Creative Head, for the Advertisement Team.' Damian introduced him to everyone. Aaron greeted everyone and took the last chair of the room which was away from the screen while Nazir sat right next to it.

'Aaron, where is Destiny?' Damian asked.

'I think she is on leave today, Sir.'

'Is she okay?'

'I hope so.' He nodded.

'Fine. I will catch her up later.' He turned to the assembly, 'Where was I?'

The meeting was being held for about forty minutes. Damian gave a speech about the company. Basically, on how it was started. SYS stands for Sell Your Shoes. Damian's first client was a shoe manufacturing company. He made it into a brand and now it is one of the successful shoe brands. Still, they do advertisements for the manufacturer with top sports persons.

'Gentlemen, Mr. Nazir has come up with an idea for your promotion. Please let him present his idea to you.'

Nazir stood up and started the presentation. The first slide alarmed Aaron. It was his research. That was not just a presentation but his three months of research on how to imply this imported product into the local market. About the product history, existing competitors, their branding ideas, and dummy ads.

Aaron was surprised to see there was no change in any slide. *What the hell? It is my idea. It's all my plan for the promotion. How could someone steal an idea and not even change the template?*

Wait a minute. He knows I was working on this but how did he get the copy? I had my file on my local disk. Darkchocolate! She too works for the Nazi.

Nazir finished his slides. Damian joined him. 'Gentlemen, as we spoke, this Thursday we are celebrating the 10th anniversary of our company. We are gladly inviting you and your General Managers. It would be a great opportunity for us to show this research and ideas to your managers. You can stay until then and explore the city.'

The foreigners nodded at him. Everyone in the room liked the presentation. It was a clear representation of branding. Aaron was not in a mood to speak about his idea. He let Nazir do whatever he wanted to do.

At least the plan wasn't wasted.

—— Chapter Eleven ——

Aaron skipped his lunch. He went directly to the pantry and took his cup from the cupboard. The cup was there for a long time and it had left a circle mark on the cupboard. He washed it once in the sink and stood before the coffee machine which he hadn't visited for like six months. Now, Destiny's absence had brought him to that machine.

He placed the cup and pressed the espresso button. The machine turned off. And restarted with a message on the red LED screen "Brewing… please wait."

'I know you are mad at me.' He spoke to the machine. It groaned twice and released hot steam on his hand.

'Hey! I'm sorry, okay? Are you giving me a coffee or not?' He yelled at the machine.

Nazir came into the pantry with a water bottle. They both froze after seeing each other. Aaron caught Nazir for stealing his idea whilst Nazir caught Aaron for talking to a coffee machine. *What? I saw someone speaking to a stool yesterday.*

'Hey, Aaron. Looks like you are angry at me?' He kept it casual.

He smiled and shook his head slowly.

'Listen, I don't know what you are thinking. But I did this for you, Son. You know, to those foreign clients, a senior's advice can be accepted quickly.'

'I can understand, Sir. Thank you, for that.' Aaron just wanted to cut the conversation.

'You won't come here usually… Where's Destiny?'

He shrugged 'As I said she is on leave today.'

'Is that why you look so sad?'

Aaron shook his head again.

Nazir chuckled, 'Don't worry about that. She will come back soon. Call her.'

Aaron walked back to his cabin holding a cup of double espresso in one hand and his phone in the other. He tried to call Destiny and still couldn't reach her. Then he called customer care to get details of last night's calls when he went out of signal. Destiny had tried to call him. *She's mad at me. She told me she will call. I have messed up. Will she talk to me again?*

Everyone who crossed him wished for his birthday. It kept breaking his thought bubbles. Destiny was right. He couldn't multi-task. He skipped everyone's conversation and reached his cabin finally.

He spotted someone sitting inside through the glass door. *Again? What does she want to steal from me now?*

'What is the matter with you?' Aaron was dumbstruck to see Damian sitting on the chair before his desk. 'Sir, I'm sorry. I thought it was someone else.'

Damian scratched his chin, 'Aaron, am I disturbing you at your break time?'

'No, Sir. It's fine.' He placed his cup on his table. 'Do you need to talk to me, Sir?'

'Have your drink. I just wanted to check you on something.' He gestured at his cup, 'Please, sit on your chair.'

'It is okay, Sir. Anything serious?'

'No, Aaron, nothing serious.' He bit his lips. 'Aaron, today you have approved all the Ad designs for the first time. The designers are happy about it. Nazir is also happy about his presentation which I know is yours. I saw the style of yours in it. Don't try to convince me. I know whatever happens in this building. I don't know why you let him take that. I'm not supposed to ask that. You made everyone happy today. I'm just concerned about… Are you happy?'

'Yes, Sir. Nazir has helped me with this. You know a senior's approach to the client can be noticed much better than mine.'

'There is no seniority in this case, Aaron. It's about innovation. You know that.'

'It's okay, Sir. Anyway, I couldn't make it happen.'

'Why? You can.' He stood up and walked to him. 'I saw that presentation. It's a really good plan. If you can plan it, you really can do it. Who else can do your idea better than you? We all are here to help you, Aaron. You should make the presentation during the anniversary event.'

'Actually sir, I won't even come to the event.'

Damian slightly threw himself back. 'How come you are not a part of the event, Aaron? You are one of the pillars of this company, I strongly believe. Tell me why. What happened?'

Aaron could come up with only one excuse. 'It's my engagement tomorrow.'

He stepped back. 'Engagement?'

'Yes, Sir. I'm going to get married.'

'Oh,' He was quiet and thinking about something for a while. 'Is that with Destiny?'

'What? Des? Destiny?' Aaron shook his head continuously. 'No, it's not her. I and Destiny? We are friends. Just friends.'

'I see,' He looked puzzled, 'So, who is your special person?'

'This is Karu. Her name is Karuvizhi and we have been in love for the last seven years.' Aaron couldn't see his face. He looked at the floor. 'I know it's new for you. I have never mentioned her to anyone in this office.'

'Yes, you have kept it very secret. Why Aaron? Aren't we that close to you?'

That question made Aaron uncomfortable. He knew that was not the reason. 'Sir, sometimes the secrets we keep might be either a humiliation or a treasure.' He lifted his face. 'And she is my treasure.'

'Uh-Huh! Shakespeare in love!' Damian smacked on Aaron's shoulders and came to hug him. 'I'm happy for you, Aaron.'

Aaron spread his hands lightly and let him hug. 'Thank you, Sir.'

Damian moved back and pointed his finger. 'But one thing. This is a condition. This event should not happen without you.'

'But, Sir, I can't.' Aaron shook.

'No excuses, Aaron.' He walked past Aaron to the door.

'I will try, Sir.' Aaron shrugged.

'You are coming,' He opened the door and held it, 'With your fiancée.'

'But, Sir, it is not possible.'

'It will. And you should. Goodbye.' He vanished from the door and it closed itself.

Aaron took a long breath. He turned to see his coffee which had lost its heat. He scratched his head and took it in his hand. He grabbed an armchair and sat against the glass wall of his room alone. Half of the city can be seen in this view. He looked beyond the city. He sat in the direction where Karu was. He wondered what she was doing.

She might be sleeping. Does that mean she is dreaming? Will she dream? Will I be in her dreams? If I will be in her dreams, the first thing I do is definitely to kiss her. The saddest thing about relationships is you really don't know which could be the last kiss. But when was it? It was not definitely when we were in the forest that night.

Oh, crap!!

Aaron just realised that night she was asking for a kiss. Their traditional game of love.

Well, it's not an expensive gift but it's a precious one. That day she actually did. She asked for it. She was being so romantic. And the whole place was romantic. A cabin in the woods, the big moon, candles, I and Karu alone. And I was being such a jerk to ask for a coffee. I think I should jump from here.

Aaron lost interest in his coffee.

Fine, when was the last kiss?

It was last Saturday, in my car while I dropped her off. The previous one, before we were arguing about her parents in the park, and before it was in a theatre. Then before that, it was in my room when everyone else in my family were too busy to notice us.

Aaron was recollecting every moment they made out together. His mind had split into two. One was in reality looking at the horizon of trees where in the middle Karu was. *And my other mind is floating on the memories of kisses. I still remember every kiss we kissed in seven years. Seven years. It's a lot of time to make kisses.*

Aaron fantasized them all in a reverse timeline in his other mind. *Then it came. The first kiss. Kiss on that terrace where we were teenagers again. That kiss made her cheeks turn red just like the inseparable reddish mud mixed with rain water.*

He clasped the coffee cup into his palms which had the slight warmth that was relevant to Karu's cheeks. *In my other mind, I'm there on that terrace holding her cheeks and kissing her.*

Then he opened his eyes and came back to reality. *My other mind disappears when the taste differs from the bittering kiss of this crappy coffee.*

After a long wait, Aaron's full week off was approved. He took his bag to leave the office. He walked out from the cabin to the corridor. The birthday wishes had never finished. He thanked back even without noticing who's wishing him.

Then he came to the elevator and waited for it to open. It was coming from the 15th floor. It opened with Destiny in front of him.

She had worn white sleeves and grey pants. She was carrying her handbag and a few papers. Her eyes seemed to be distracted.

'Des?'

She looked so tired. 'Are you coming in?'

'Yeah.'

She waved him to get in and he entered the elevator and it closed. They were alone. And it was quiet except for the elevator music. She didn't say anything. But he needed to.

'Err_' He wanted to point at her phone. But she had no phone in her hands. *It's weird.*

She asked, 'Did you come to say something?'

'Yes, I tried to call you.'

'Oh, my phone. I kept it in my apartment.' She made a fuss.

'Alright. When did you come?' he asked.

'Just an hour ago. Leaving now.'

'Okay… Did you look at the group chat?'

'No, I'm really busy. Actually, it's my day off. I came to get some paperwork.'

'Yeah, I can see,' he nodded. He had nothing to ask more. His mind was blank. He felt a sudden change in his relationship with her. *It was not a discovered relationship. Yet it was good. A good companionship. What made a difference to it?*

'Aaron!'

'Yes?'

'You came to my apartment on Saturday. Right?' She asked.

'Yes, I did.' He nodded.

'Did you see any pendant that is shaped like a star?'

'Oh!' Aaron pretended like he was thinking although he was thinking. *Where the hell did I lose that?*

He shrugged, 'I don't know. Is it important?'

'No, it's okay. Thank you, Aaron.'

If it isn't important, then why is she asking me? She is reminding me of my arrival on that day. She is definitely angry with me. But why this much? She knew it is my birthday. Yet not wishing me.

The elevator came to the ground floor. It opened. 'Okay, see you around, Aaron.' She left the elevator.

'Hey, wait...' Aaron came out and stopped her.

She turned to him with a questioning look. 'Do you want to say anything?'

'Yes, I need to tell you something.'

'Fire it away, then.'

'Ahh, it's...'

'It's?' She looked at her watch.

Looking at the watch. It is her classic move to brush off people. This is not weird to me. Because this is how Destiny treats everyone else in the office. Now I can see why they all hate her. I want to tell her I'm sorry, but I'm embarrassed to tell her. Okay! Let me say it is my birthday.

'It is my engagement tomorrow.'

'Oh,' she kept quiet for a moment. Then said, 'Congratulations!' she smiled. 'But I'm really sorry I have some work tomorrow. I can't come to your engagement.'

Why did I inform her that? All of sudden? Does that mean I have conveyed to her we have nothing to speak about anymore?

'Yeah, that's okay.'

'See you then.' She smirked and turned back to leave.

What's the matter with her? I once didn't wish Karu on her birthday still she didn't show any anger towards me. And this is the first year ever since I was 12, Karu hasn't wished me on this day. I don't think anyone could be in her place. And this Destiny, 'She's not that worthy,' words came out from him.

He grimaced and walked back to the car.

—— Chapter Twelve ——

Aaron slept for a few hours in the night. He had a blurry dream. He was with Karu again in that cabin. This time they were happy. He could see her eyes. She was laughing with her sparkling teeth. It was just a twenty seconds' dream. He woke up. Then the rest of the night went thinking, *was that really Karu?*

He went out early in the morning to go jogging. He came back home, clean shaven and with a much-needed haircut. After a hot shower, his muscle sores were better.

Aaron looked at his new look in his mirror. He had suited up in a new midnight blue single-breasted suit and trousers with notch lapels under a linen white shirt. A maroon striped tie added more style. *Is this what you always wanted me to look like, Karu?*

'You look so handsome, son.' Aaron's mother appeared in his mirror leaning on his room doorway. 'If today is a normal engagement no girl would say no to your proposal.'

'Thanks, mom, everyone's ready?' He turned to her, wearing polished black shoes.

Mrs. Stitch had dressed in a royal blue long gown and applied her face cream. Her brown hairs were puffed up into a bun with a few bangs. 'Yes, children are having breakfast. Come and join us.'

'But mom, it's getting late. We have to leave now.' Aaron's loud voice boomed in the living room. Mr. Stitch was relaxing on his couch with black coffee in a cup in one hand and a pen with a newspaper in another. 'Dad! What are you doing?'

He shrugged, 'It's Tuesday, son. Crossword puzzles.'

'I know that.'

'Then help me with this. "Everyone's favourite movie genre. We see twice of whom we paid for." What could be that genre?' He sipped his coffee.

'Dad, we have to leave by now.' He yelled.

'Look, Aaron, I'm ready.' He gestured at his black Tuxedo with a white shirt and a red bow tie on his collar. 'Stella and Edward have to finish their breakfast. I will complete this before they come.'

'Ed! Stella! It's getting late. What are you guys doing?' Aaron shifted his voice to the dining table. He noticed Stella was eating French toast. 'Woah! Why have you dressed like Karu?'

'It's her engagement too.' She shrugged. She was dressed in a red Kurti with blue neck designs decorated with gemstones, above her denim pants.

Aaron's mom came to him with a plate of French toasts. 'Aaron, eat this,'

'Mom, Egg! I will smell of egg. And I don't have time. We have to leave by now.' He checked the time under his cuffs. 'Stella, can't you eat faster? Where's Ed?' He noticed Edward, which made him laugh. 'Why are you dressed like Karu, Ed?'

Edward was wiping his hands with a towel. He threw it away, kicking the floor ajith his brown pointy shoe. 'Stella insisted me to wear this.'

Stella hooted, 'It's called kurta! It's for boys too.' She finished her breakfast. 'You boys don't know anything about fashion.'

Edward dressed in a cyan Kurta embroidered with white little balls and white pants. He raised a beige scarf from the chair. 'Look, Aaron. Do I have to wear this too?'

Aaron laughed again. 'It's okay. At least you are ready. Let's move.'

'No, I'm going to change. Dad gave me a new Tux. I will go and get ready.' Edward rushed to his room.

Stella got up and followed him. 'Ed! We talked about this. Don't do anything stupid.'

His mother came with a plate. 'Aaron, here is your sandwich. You only left. Have this.'

'Mom!' He shouted, 'Can you all understand what I'm saying here? We have to be there at 11 AM. Now it is 10 already.'

The mother pleased him, 'Just a sandwich. How long will it take? Eat fast.'

'Darla, "Everyone's favourite movie genre. We see twice of whom we paid for." What's that?' Mr. Stitch asked, scratching his head with a pen.

'How many letters, Howard?' She asked.

'Eight boxes can hold.'

'Mom! Dad!' Aaron tried to get his parents' attention. But their other children got it.

Stella ran from Edward from their room with his Tuxedo. 'Ed! Stop right there.' She grabbed a ketchup bottle from the dining table. 'If you come closer, I will pour the sauce in this. This thick and delicious sauce can spoil your day.'

Edward stopped chasing her. 'Mom, look at what she is doing?'

Aaron yelled, 'What is the matter with you, Stella? Let him wear what he wants.'

'It will take more time to change. Is it okay for you?' Stella jerked back when Ed tried to snatch it from her hands. 'Ed!' She threatened him with widened eyes, 'Move back! Or I will destroy this. Listen to your twin sister.'

'Oh, the twins. Howard! It's dual role,' the mother went to help with crossword puzzles.

'Okay! Stop this! Everyone! Listen!' Aaron shouted and got the attention he wanted. 'Look, we have to be there at 11. It's not a matter of how late you make. I will drive fast enough to be there at 11. So, if you guys don't want to throw up in the car, get your asses in the car. Now!'

Everyone went silent until Mr. Stitch clanked his coffee cup on the table. He stood up barefoot and walked to Aaron. 'Look, young man. I need to inform you about something.'

Aaron and others listened to him seriously.

'I'm getting the passenger seat today.' He informed and rushed to pick his shoes. He vanished from the house.

'No! I want to sit in the front!' Ed followed him.

'Me too!' Stella picked his scarf and ran with him. Aaron turned to his mother holding the plate.

'Don't stare at me like that. I will pack this. You can eat in the car.'

Everyone became calm in the car. Aaron ate breakfast while driving on the way to Karu's. Aaron's car is not a comfortable ride for a family. His mother was shrunken in-between Stella and Edward, both got window seats in the back. In front, his father Howard Stitch was closing his eyes and feeling the wind. Like a promotion day, he felt proud of this stage of his life.

Howard never went to school. He hadn't remembered any events with his father. His mother had told him that most of his ancestors were tailors. That was how they got the family name. Although he hadn't met any of those Stitchs', he developed a passion for tailoring clothes. He admired the structure of people only for the clothes they wear. That made him start up his own cloth store for suits.

Now Aaron was wearing the suit he stitched by his hands the last day in his office. It suited Aaron very well. On recalling from scratch to this point, he was proud of sitting in his son's car and going for his engagement.

Aaron's phone rang. A call from Karu's number. He attended the call without any knowledge of the phone linked with Car's sound system.

Cara spoke in Karu's voice, 'Hey Aaron, Karu's mother asked me to check where you have reached by now. Are you on your way?'

'Why is she saying Karu's mother? It's her mother, right?' Aaron's mother was confused.

'She is nervous, mom. Don't ask her questions.' Stella yelled, 'Karu, we are on our way. Don't worry, I will be there soon.'

Aaron unlinked the phone from the car, 'We will be in a few minutes, Kar…u… Karu. Tell them we are on our way. Your parents. Yeah… Bye.'

Ed asked, 'Are they living in the suburbs?'

'Yes, but not so far.' Aaron pointed through the window, 'This was our school. So, we are halfway through.'

Edward leaned on the window and looked at the crossing school. It didn't look fancy like his school. He started to think of Aaron and Karu. *This is where it all started years ago. The love story of Aaron and Karu. How do they still love each other? They didn't even break up once. Kids of my age are breaking up and moving to another person easily. I have no friends who have this one love forever relationship. If my brother and Karu had broken up because of the trouble they had, I might have stopped believing that relationship exists. They won't. They are engaging today. I wish I would get that one love forever in my life too. Like the only living proof, Aaron and Karu. Made for each other.*

Maybe today I can get to meet any cousins of my future sister-in-law.

'Aaron. Did you book the van?' His mother asked.

'What van?'

'I told your father to tell you to pick up our relatives from the city hall. Did he tell you?'

'No, he didn't.' Aaron shook his head.

'Howard? Didn't you tell him?'

Aaron checked at him, 'He has slept, Mom.'

'Oh, god. Our relatives! They are standing in the street. With babies in their hands. Please, anybody, make something.'

Mr. Stitch opened his eyes and winked at Aaron and went back to sleep.

'Dad!' Aaron sighed. 'Edward. Book a cab from your phone. Mom, how many of them are waiting there?'

Mom replied, 'How do I know? They are like three families.'

'Ed, book three SUVs and select pay on the drop.' Aaron checked at his father who winked at him again and pretended to sleep.

Stella wasn't listening to them. She had put her chin on the window sill and looked at the crossing trees of that suburban area. The valleys and mountains following behind them. She wanted to slide down the window and smell the tamarind leaves. But it would spoil her hair for the day.

Stella always wanted a sister. With whom she could share all of her thoughts. Her mother couldn't understand her as she wanted. She wanted a friendly sister with whom she can share dresses, nail paints, and her homework loads. She was happy about Karu coming to her house. And she was excited about this engagement. She could hardly wait for the time to change rings.

'Aaron, did you see the ring?' Stella asked him.

'No, you bought it. Right?' He asked sceptically.

'Ugh! Aaron! It's your engagement. Be a little more excited. Look at this. Now.' She showed him a golden ring in a maroon box.

Aaron checked it from the rear mirror, 'That's good. Looking nice. Are you sure they would have bought gold too?'

She rolled her eyes, 'Yes, I'm sure. That's the tradition.'

Tradition! This word hit on Mrs. Stitch's mind. *What kind of tradition is it that they have never spoken to me or Howard yet? Do they know that Aaron has parents? First of all, why should we pay attention to them? Have they given birth to a girl who can't be found anywhere in the world? I know Karu isn't so special. But I like her. In fact, I'm doing all this for her. If there would be any person other than Karu, I won't accept these things to happen.*

Aaron's mind had only one thought in loop mode. *It is not my Karu.*

'Howard, did you get the gift?' The mother asked.

Aaron turned to see him sleeping. 'Dad, did you get the gift? We can't buy anything here. Dad?'

'Yes, he did,' Edward said, 'I saw a gift box in the frunk. But I don't know what it is.'

'Dad, I know you are not really sleeping. Tell us what that gift is.' Aaron poked him. 'Dad!'

'He is sleeping for real.' Mrs. Stitch said.

'No, he isn't.' Aaron yelled. 'I saw him winking at me.'

Edward and Stella leaned forward to check on their father. Edward said, 'No one could tell the difference.'

Stella joined, 'Yeah, that's dad.'

Finally, they had reached Karu's house. A group of Karu's relatives and a band of musicians dressed in the red and white uniform of drums and trumpets were welcoming the family.

Everyone there was waiting to see how the groom looked. To fill their expectations, Aaron stepped out of the mustang and looked at everyone. There were no familiar faces to him.

A video camera in a man's shoulder was filming him from the car's entry. His family got out and stood beside him.

'Are they from foreign?' Someone in the group asked about seeing the costumes of Aaron's parents. Then Stella and Edward found no one wearing Kurtas there. It's all churidars, sarees, shirts, and dhotis.

Aaron stood there with his overdressed family members. The whole family felt alienated here.

—— Chapter Thirteen ——

Clem was sitting at a table outside a café where they allowed her to smoke. She lit her third cigarette of the day and gazed at the street, cars, and people. The noise of the city annoyed her so much. If she had a body with the strength of an elephant, she would have knocked them all and destroyed the place to dust.

They were coming to her. Slowly from the midpoint of the core. The images developed in her mind as though the sorrows. It felt like someone else's sorrows. But the pain lifted up was real. The more she brought up the more she was broken. Her mind was not anymore indistinct. She had discovered more than what she should have known.

The most strengthening thing one can do is knowing themselves. Clem dived deep into the stream of darkest waters, reached the doomed cave and opened the glowing chest of truth. She got the strength of a thousand elephants from the truth she discovered.

The awakening made her blow out all the griminess she had in her mind with those grey smoke. There was only one thing left on the top of her mind. That filled throughout the lowermost. That was revenge.

Aaron and his family received a warm welcome from Karu's family as soon as they entered, they saw the entrance decorated with banana trees and mango leaves.

Karu's father wearing a yellow silk shirt and white dhoti gladly welcomed Aaron's family.

Aaron introduced his family to them, 'Uh… These are my parents. And Edward… This is Stella. My brother and sister.'

'Come inside.' Karu's mom gave them a full smile that was different from what she showed a day ago to Aaron.

The shoes and slippers were left on the doorway floor. Stella removed her shoes. Aaron stood in confusion.

'It is okay, you can wear it.' Karu's mom said. She brought them to their living room. Karan welcomed them with a nod. Then he told the cameraman to give them a rest.

Aaron sat on a single person sofa. Karu's father sat on the sofa against him. His family sat together on a long one in the middle. They all looked weird like they had come to the wrong house. The coffee table was filled with sweets and spiral savories. They kept giving smiles to people who greeted them.

Stella tapped on the dancing head of a classical dancer woman doll on the stand beside her. 'This is awesome.'

Aaron glared at her 'Stella!'

Edward looked at the paintings on the wall around them, 'Are these hand-painted?'

'Yes, we bought it from the antique artists.' Karu's mom placed a tray of brown coffees in stainless-steel cups.

'You have a very beautiful house,' Aaron's mom started the conversation, 'And the furniture is all good wood. My father used to be a carpenter. So, I can say. They are well-finished work.'

'It's all been here for almost 30 years. My husband varnishes it regularly.'

'Well, that's so good,' Mr. Stitch handed the gift box to Karu's Father, 'It's a little gift from the Stitch family.'

'Thank you. This is my elder son, Karan.'

'Oh, Karan.' He nodded, 'And by the way, I was about to ask your family name,' he trailed off when Aaron shook his head. 'It's good to see you all.'

Karu's father handed the gift to Karan, 'Keep this inside.'

'Make yourself comfortable. The stage is getting ready. I will go and take a look at that.' Karu's father walked out. They all were relieved a little.

In front of Aaron, Karan opened the gift from the dining room. 'Dad, what's the gift?'

He smiled. 'It's a 35–year-old special whiskey.' He smirked and his fingers were saying super.

Aaron slapped his head. Stella whispered, 'Daddy! You should not give drinks in a traditional ceremony. No one drinks here.'

'No drinks?' he asked sceptically. 'Oh no!'

Aaron checked on Karan who opened the gift, put it on the dining table, and walked away to his room in upset. 'Thanks, dad.'

Aaron walked to the kitchen and Karu's mom checked the gift. 'I'm sorry.' *What else I could say?*

'No, problem. You please keep this in Karu's room upstairs? Our guests will take it wrong when they see it here. We have more problems than you think.'

'Sure. I'm sorry about that.'

He took that and walked out of the dining room. His family was all busy tasting the coffee and snacks. Aaron climbed the stairs.

'Dad, try this.' Edward showed him a spherical yellow sweet.

'Wait, this coffee is amazing!' He enjoyed the aromatic coffee, 'What type of brewing is this?'

'That's called filter coffee.' Stella had became a full-time guide.

Aaron stopped at Karu's room. He felt memories of him sneaking into this room with his shoes. He knocked at the door and waited for a response.

'Who's there?' Karu's voice made a louse in his heart.

'Aaron here.' He wished the voice should come from Karu when the door opens.

The door opened with a wet hand. Cara was standing in the doorway with only a pink towel wrapped around her body and another white towel tied on her hair. 'Hey!' She sounded excited to see him.

Aaron was drawn into her looking like this. She looked like Karu, sounded like Karu and now he noticed she also smelled exactly like Karu. He saw Karu's face without her eyeliner. He tried to get rid of his eyes on her. *Wait, it is Karu's body. I can see it. Can't I?*

'What? Why are you looking like that? You know who I am?' She tied her arms and leaned on the wall.

'Sorry,' he shook his head, 'Can you keep this inside?' He handed her the bottle. Her hands had mehndi designs from her fingertips to her forearms.

She kept it on the table. Aaron got to see water drops on her shoulders. 'Uh... Everything's okay here?'

She turned back, 'Yeah, okay. I think I'm doing good as Karu. What about you?'

'I'm good.' He nodded, 'And, is Karu alright?'

She leaned her head on the wall. 'For sure. You don't have to worry. She will be good and come back soon. Then you can gaze at her all day.'

'I don't have any idea how I'm going to deal with that. I mean what shall I tell her? How can I explain all these?' He scratched his frown.

'I can understand. We will figure this out. I will help when that happens. I will be there. She can… Believe things.'

He nodded without a word.

'Karu!' Karu's mother reacted shocked to see them together. 'What are you doing? Go inside!'

Aaron was puzzled. Cara vanished inside before he turned to her. Her mother came to the door, 'Get ready soon.'

'Look, Aaron. You should not meet Karu like this before marriage. Okay? I'm like your mother now. Listen to me, wait until the marriage. Today is only the engagement and it's so soon. You know that.'

'I'm sorry. I'm going downstairs.'

'And you will be staying in this room tonight. We have arranged a guest room for your family. Is that okay?'

'Yes, okay. Everything is okay.' He nodded multiple times. He got down from the stairs and took a wrong turn that ended in their backyard. He looked around the garden of neem trees and some flower plants.

'Maaahh!' He was frozen to hear a mooing and bell sounds behind him. He turned to see a bull before him. It was huge and muscled. The curved horns were sharp like a pencil. It swung its tail like a giant monster smashing buildings. It came towards him.

A big pot-bellied man came there and pulled the rope tied on its nose. 'Don't be scared, brother. Come on, come here.' He invited Aaron under the roof. Aaron stepped carefully from the cow dung on the ground. 'Touch here.'

The man touched its forehead and insisted Aaron to try. Aaron took his hand close to it. It was chewing and drooling but sharply staring at Aaron. A strong blow of air came out from the bull that scared him. 'It's okay, I will touch him some other day.' Aaron rushed out from that place.

Karu's father brought his in-laws to the neighbouring land which belongs to him. He had built a stage with red carpet and flower decorations. The roof was decorated with bright rice lights hanging in waves. The background of the stage had placed texts saying, "Engagement of Aaron Stitch H. And Karuvizhi K."

Before the stage, there were plastic chairs arranged in between a red carpet that meets the stage. Aside from the stage, there were four long rows of dining tables where people eating and serving were happening. Karu's father advised them to eat first.

They all were sitting in a row. Aaron sat in a corner seat beside his mother and his father between Edward and Stella.

And the lunch meals were full of boiled rice and varieties of gravies and vegetable fries and crisps. Aaron and his family were already familiar with Karu's cooking. So, the food was not so strange for them. The strange thing was the videographer capturing them eating. They all froze for a moment and looked weirdly at the camera. Mrs. Stitch asked, 'Is that proof of what we ate?'

'Mom, don't look at the camera. Act normally.' Stella sipped water and turned to see the rest of the family staring at her.

After eating lunch, Karu's father brought Aaron to the stage. He said they had to wait until the good time comes to exchange rings and advised them to make the reception.

He stood on the stage facing the guest sitting on the chairs. Everyone was passing comments on how he looked. It sounded like standing on the sea shore. Odd thing is, Aaron couldn't feel the breeze. They played songs that are similar to Karu's playlist. It remembered him of her.

I really want to see Karu.

—— Chapter Fourteen ——

It was anxious for Aaron to stand on the stage alone while strangers were watching him sweating. He wanted to relax. He tried listening to an old song playing there. It turned out he was liking it. He even hummed a little while looking around.

Cara appeared at the end of the aisle walking to the stage. She was wearing a glossy purple silk saree with a green blouse. Both hands were drawn on mehndi, eyeliners highlighted Karu's eyes, lip gloss, and pieces of jewellery like necklace, bangles, and more Aaron couldn't name them.

Karu's parents made her appear like she was born for this day. Aaron was stunned to see her like this. He never thought Karu is this beautiful. Cara looked at his stunned look on her. She lifted her eyebrows to ask what. He shook his head.

His mind went blank. But he insisted himself saying, *it is not my Karu. It is not my Karu. It is not my Karu.*

Guests were coming on stage and taking photos with them like a wedding reception. Aaron's parents couldn't tolerate the fact that they were not at an actual wedding yet. They were more relieved when their relatives finally arrived.

Aaron had to introduce his guests to her and her as Karu to them. He did. And Cara did the same. She touched her guests she didn't know and read their memory to introduce them to Aaron.

'This is my teacher, remember once I showed you a pen she gifted?' Cara introduced a woman in her 50s.

'Uh?' Aaron was freaked out.

'Forgot?' She was doing Karu's expressions.

'Yes, it was a nice pen.' He smiled at the teacher.

'Nice selection, Karu. Congrats to you both.' The teacher grinned at both.

It was good Aaron hadn't invited his neighbours. Because he didn't know their names. Unlike Aaron, Cara introduced him to Karu's whole neighbourhood who were close to her family. Aaron was secretly counting how many of them have to beat up him if they find out who she is and what really happened to Karu.

'This is my favourite uncle. Remember me saying once I broke his rib as a child?' That was the topmost memory Cara could find from a middle-aged uncle of Karu. He and Aaron exchanged awkward silence for a second.

'Wow, she has remembered everything. It happened when she was 5.' He told Aaron. 'You are a lucky person, man. Be careful when you lie to her.' He laughed and posed for the photo.

Aaron looked freaked out in that photo. *I want to scream to them all "It is not my Karu!" This whole place is alienated.*

Then one of Aaron's cousin sisters came up to the stage. She shook Cara's hand and congratulated her with a smile. Cara smiled back and told Aaron, 'This is Daisy, a schoolmate of my college mate, Riya. We met once at Riya's baby shower. Also, a fashion designer'

'Also, my cousin Daisy,' he mimicked her.

'Oh!' She met Cousin Daisy's confused eyes, 'Then you are from both sides,' she grinned at her.

'I'm so glad that you recognized me.' Cousin Daisy grinned back. She still doubted how could Karu knew she was a fashion designer. That happened just a few months before. Then the photographer distracted her thoughts. She posed for the photo.

After she walked out, Aaron whispered 'Whoa, you are going too much. Please stop this.' He loosened his tie a little.

'What?' she shrugged, 'Everything is going well. Don't worry.'

A group of Edward and Stella's classmates came in kurtas and half sarees with them on the stage. They filled the stage and the camera screen. They took a selfie on Stella's phone covering everyone. Aaron was confused when his siblings invited them all. And why?

At last, the good time came. Both families gathered on stage except Karan. His mother had tried to bring him. But he went to make an important call.

It came time to exchange the rings. Karu's father gave Cara a golden ring. Aaron felt something wrong with what was happening. *It is not my Karu. How can I accept a ring from someone or something other than Karu? And even I have to do the ring. This doesn't seem fair. I can't engage with it. It looks like Karu. But I know it is not Karu. Now, it smiles and shows its hand to me. It's the same hand. I can spot the mole on her wrist. Still, my mind keeps saying that it is not my Karu. I need to stop this.*

'Stop this!'

All faces turned to the aisle. It was from a middle-aged lady who walked on the carpet with her son and a daughter beside her.

'What is going on here?' Aaron's mother asked.

Karu's father responded, 'Wait, it's our relative. It's my nephew and niece. We will talk.'

That middle-aged woman who is an aunt for Karu was throwing strong words at Karu's father, 'What is going on here? An engagement? Everyone here knows who is fixed to your daughter. It's my son. Don't you remember?'

'Please, we can talk.' Karu's father tried to calm her.

'What is more to talk about? All of a sudden you have arranged this engagement. You said your son can't marry my daughter. Because she is dumb.' She pointed at her daughter, Hema, who is verbally challenged from birth. 'But you promised us that your daughter is fixed for my son.'

Now, Aaron got an idea of who they are. Karu has told him this story. *If I didn't come into Karu's life she would have married this guy already.*

'What's going on, son?' His father asked.

'Dad, wait. Let them talk first.'

'Tell my children an answer and then continue this engagement.'

'But… My daughter likes this boy. And he seems to keep her happy. I'm apologizing for not telling you. But please let this happen now. We will talk about this for sure,' He folded his hands before her.

'I'm not going anywhere until I get an answer from you. Let me see how you make this. Who are they? Do they relate to any of us? Don't you think it's a shame to our culture?'

'Okay, this lady is speaking too much. I'm going to speak to her.' Aaron's mother stepped forward.

'Mom, no. Wait!' Aaron yelled and stopped her.

'You, wait here, aunty, I will take care of this.' Cara said.

'What? What are you going to do?' Aaron yelled at her but she already walked out of the stage. 'Stop, don't go there.'

Cara walked to Karu's Aunt and stood before her quietly for a moment. Aaron looked closer; she was holding her hands.

'I'm sorry to hurt your feelings. It is not my father's fault. It was me who wished to marry this person. And also, you are like another mother to me. I don't want to become your daughter-in-law. Please bless me as your daughter.' She fell on her foot to ask for a blessing.

The aunt was speechless for a while and then lifted her. Then Cara moved to her son and placed her hand on his shoulder. 'Do you remember the time we used to play behind your house? All the time you were like a caring brother to me? How can I think of marrying you?' she squinted her eyes, 'Can you?'

He put his face down in guilt. Aaron was shocked to see his silence. *What is it doing?*

Then his sister, Hema, said something in her sign language. Cara hugged her and replied something in sign language. She motioned her fist on her heart and pointed at Aaron. Then pointed at Aaron and motioned on her heart. She signed to say, "What else could be a better reason to make a promise fail?"

The girl was speechless. Maybe sign-less. She just shrugged away. Most of the guests were filled with tears. Two persons knew that it was a drama. One was Karan who made a call to his aunt to report the engagement. And Aaron knew the exact truth of who was making all these. *What has happened here? Why is it making this scene? Karu won't do this. Karu has no idea about sign language.*

Aaron's father was filled with tears on seeing these. 'Son, you are so lucky to have a girl like her.'

'Dad? You too… What?'

The lady and her children apologized to Karu's parents and they all were coming back to the stage. Everyone was filled with mixed emotions of happiness and tears. Aaron was confused. *Is this all these people want? Just some melodrama? Like some TV soap? Is that what I'm lacking?*

'Humanity has no language, son.' Aaron's father said in his observation, 'Love is the language of all. It has no shape. No colour and no discrimination. You did something serious that has brought you things you wished for. Thanks for doing it for us too.'

Aaron couldn't say anything. He stood quietly there until everything came back to normal. Cara showed her hand again at him. He was thinking about what his father said earlier.

'Aaron!' his father whispered, 'Ask her.'

Aaron took a breath. 'Karu, if you didn't come into my life, I would be blind. What I see would be only darkness. You saved me from dark. And your love never let me to experience it. You taught me that love has no shape or colour. It's a light. Sometimes we need sentiments in life. Have to believe in things that have no prospect. Cannot be rational in everything. We are made up of emotions. There is no wrong to let our pride go away for it. Now here, I'm almost marrying you, Karu. Wherever you are, my heart always find you. I hope this will go to you. Will you take me, Karu?'

Cara acted like she ran into tears on his speech. She was familiar with the stage. She maintained what the audience wanted to see. She gave them the show of a typical girl expressing during a proposal. She nodded emotionally, 'Yes!'

Aaron slipped the ring in Cara's finger and she did the same with Aaron. They were engaged, Aaron and Karuvizhi, in front of both families and their relatives, friends, and neighbours.

The marriage date was announced. It was six months later. Aaron was relieved to think that marriage would happen with the original Karu. He looked into her face. He knew it was not Karu. Still, he wanted to see it.

His mother moved slowly to Karu's mom and asked something in her ears. Karu's mom's lips turned into a line and she shook her head slowly. Aaron knew what his mother asked. *Okay, this is embarrassing.*

A trumpet sound followed by drums made everyone turn at the entrance. The band people with trumpets and drums marched on the carpet and followed by them a group of kurtas dancing led by Edward and Stella. They stood frozen before the stage and moved in rhythm one by one.

Aaron was shocked. Then he realized Stella's plan of a dance performance for the day. The music made others move their muscles.

Then a few young persons from Karu's relatives joined the performance. Parents were pushing their children to join in the dance. Stella ran to the stage and pulled Aaron and Karu. Aaron stayed back. Cara went to join them. She learned dance steps from Stella and danced with her.

No! No, Karu doesn't know dancing! Aaron was agitated that no one found it weird. Then Edward came to the stage and pushed Aaron to the dancing group.

Aaron started to move. Those were simple moves but grew fast. He was dancing to the drum sounds in his suits. That made everyone cheer with him. The whole place went on celebration of music.

The beats got faster; everyone danced fast energetically. Aaron's eyes spot the stage background letters. The name of his and Karu's. For a short period, he had forgotten it was not Karu. His moves went slow. His eyes filled with tears. He wished this all to happen with Karu. He moved from that place. He wanted to walk somewhere alone.

Then a hand clenched his wrist. He turned to see Cara holding him. No one noticed them in the rumble of music and celebration. Karu's parents were enjoying Mr. Stitch's moves.

Cara noticed his eyes. Cara looked into his eyes. She didn't need to read his memories this time, she could understand his pain. Aaron threw off her hand and walked out of the place.

—— Chapter Fifteen ——

'**I**s Aaron okay?'

Karu's mother was serving dinner for both families after their guests left the house. 'Shall we call him?'

Aaron's mother replied, 'Yes, he said he is having head pain. Just tired. We shall let him sleep.'

'Oh then, Karu, take a plate and give it to him in the room.' Karu's mother called Cara, but she felt guilty about meeting Aaron.

'Why me?'

'Karu,' she grunted.

'I think he is okay.' Aaron's father interjected, 'Aaron is kind of a persistent person... You know? If he says he is not hungry, no one can make him eat.'

'Okay, then. Karan said he will eat in the room. Don't think anything wrong. He usually eats in his room.'

'It is okay. All the talkative persons are here.' Howard smiled at Karu's father who forced a smile back.

'What is this?' Cara asked at her plate. Karu's mother placed four idlies topped with ghee and chilli powder.

'You don't know?' Karu's mother asked.

'Yes, this looks like a spicy version of *idli*. Or anything new?' Edward asked.

'It is called *Podi Idli*. Same. We also have *chapatis* and string hoppers. Try gravies too.'

Cara tasted the *idlies*. 'Mmmm.... It is wonderful. Also, spicy. I love it.'

'Karu, you have eaten those like a thousand times.'

'So what? It is the first time with us. And also,' Aaron's father took his glass of water and gave a toast, 'Today we are gathered for our first dinner. This day will glow in our mind whenever we step into this house.'

Stella whispered to Cara, 'He is best at making toasts.' Cara smirked and continued to eat. She put more idlies and gravies to fill her alien tummy.

'We are so happy to engage our son in a family like yours. This traditional engagement is new for us. We all felt nervous about how it would go. But we really enjoyed the occasion. And the important thing is, we came to know that marriage is not only between a bride and groom. We came to know you all, you all came to know us. It's been a pleasure to be welcomed by you. I'm so glad that Aaron has found the right girl for himself and for us.' He nodded at Cara. He was thinking of a family name to finish his toast, 'To... Karu's family!'

'I'm waiting for his toast on your marriage,' Stella said. Then it occurred to her, 'So! What about marriage? Will it be traditional too?'

Karu's father said, 'Actually, yes. We are supposed to marry in a temple. In our traditional way.'

'Oh! Again traditional?' Aaron's mother sounded opposing, 'But we would like to make the marriage happen in the church. What do you say, Howard?'

'Huh? I don't know. What is the name of this?' He pointed to a dish on his plate.

'Why don't we have two weddings on the same day?' Edward said with food in his cheeks, 'Favours both sides.'

'Ed! How could you come up with a wonderful idea like that? That would be wonderful!' Stella was excited, 'Mom, imagine us dressed in traditional and also,' She turned to Karu's father, 'Uncle, you will look handsome in a tuxedo. I can't wait for the day.'

Aaron's mother doesn't feel good about this. 'This is not fair_'

'That sounds good.' Howard held his wife's hand under the table and nodded at her. 'Right, Darla?'

Darla shrugged, 'Yes, that will be nice.'

Meanwhile, in Karu's room, Aaron was walking barefoot, sleeplessly. He hung his blazer on the chair in front of Karu's desk. He was in the same white shirt with sleeves folded below his elbows and same pants. The tie was hanging loosely around his neck. That room held a strong memory of Aaron's desire for Karu. He could feel her all over the room. The bed reminded him of the limited romance during his sneak peeks in the past. The bathroom attached to the room was filled with Karu's soap scent. *Is that soap's fragrance or does the soap get her fragrance? Definitely, a new pack won't have this scent.*

He wanted a distraction. He looked around Karu's bookshelf. It was full of poetry books. Then he opened the bottom cupboard of the shelf. There he found a few packets of sanitary napkins and a shoebox. He took out the box and sat on the floor. He opened the box. It was full of letters and gifts that Aaron had given to Karu over the years.

There was a little box that had a silver ring Aaron had bought by saving his pocket money, a pink panda toy, a guitar-shaped purple watch that was not working, three empty bottles of nail paints, his passport-sized photo of when he was 19. And, the letters he wrote for her, drafts of unsent letters she wrote for him, and a few sticky note papers with one-line sayings once Aaron had slipped them in her school bag.

Aaron took a deep breath after seeing all those gifts. Everyone hides a treasure within themselves. Aaron was Karu's and Karu was Aaron's.

Aaron sat on her desk with the unsent letters. He poured the whiskey his father bought, in a pencil cup Karu had. He opened a box of nuts and dry fruits from the stack of gift boxes. He chewed some almonds and drank. He looked into Karu's handwriting, he remembered every little curve of her writing. It made him travel back in time. The time when he was in this room with her. Time always acted weirdly to them, whenever they met it never was enough. During that time Karu kept him hidden in her palms but when the time came, she had to let him go.

Dear Aaron,

When you were here in my room, I was prepared to say many things. But words are not coming out in place to form a sentence. You always ask me why I'm not looking at you. If I look at you it makes me cry. I want to be with you all the time like this. I won't let you go if I look at you. When we are cuddling, I went to thousands of heavens and came back because you were not there in all those places. You cast me the spell to not talk, you made me fall completely for you. I love you, Aaron. Please make me a promise you won't leave me in any period of our life. It should be "our life" forever. Even I can feel your warmth and smell on me. Hugging myself here, I'm missing you so much.

Yours Karu.

That room held a lot of memories than he thought. Aaron was missing Karu like never before.

Everyone was sleeping peacefully after a long, tiresome day. The house sounded of only snorts and movement of a coconut tree erected from the ground. It waved its head of long and thick green leaves at the waning gibbous moon. *I need to see Karu now.*

Like a magnetic pull from the moon, he walked to the balcony. There he found Karu standing and looking at the moon. Her hair glowed partly in the moonlight. It was a replica of the phase it had in the sky. The tree nodded its head in the air. The breeze made Aaron shiver indicating that was not a dream. He went closer to grab her into him.

'Karu!'

She turned, 'It's me, Cara.'

Disappointment hit Aaron and shattered all of his emotions. 'What are you doing here?'

'I couldn't sleep. I thought to come in to check on you. Are you okay?'

He nodded, 'Let's go inside. If Karan saw you like this he will create a scene.' He walked into the room. Cara stopped at the doorway on the balcony. 'What?'

'I sense some powerful memories here.' She felt disturbed.

'Yeah, me too. Whiskey?' He showed her the bottle.

'No, I don't need it.'

'Alright, then take a seat.' He poured another round of drink in the cup and sat on the edge of the bed.

Cara was thinking deep, sitting beside him. 'I'm sorry, Aaron.'

'For?' He sipped his drink.

'Everything. This should be Karu. She should be here. This engagement is the most special day of her life. She missed it. And I really don't know how will you going to explain all this to her.'

He finished the cup and poured again, 'Really! Really, I don't know.' He spread his arms, 'And I miss her so much. I want to be with her.' He leaned forward, 'Shall we go now.'

'Not now. We shall go in the morning.'

'Alright.' He leaned back, 'And also, thanks.'

'For?' She asked.

'Everything.' Aaron sounded boozed.

'Everything? I thought everything I did was just troubling you.'

'At least I have you now. Thanks for being here.' He took a long sigh that smelled of the whiskey, 'At least I have you now.'

'As a friend?' She asked.

Aaron smiled and nodded 'You know? Cara means friend.'

'Oh! I didn't know that. Thanks.' Cara said. Aaron nodded slowly and thought of Karu.

'I'm sorry about what I said. That you don't want Karu and that's because of Destiny. I take back my words.'

'That's okay… You know this happens in long term relationships. Someone new will enter in our life like friends, co-workers who we meet every day and who knows us better than our lovers. But that doesn't replace people in our hearts.'

'Great talk,' she nodded. 'So, tell me something about you and Karu.'

'What you want to know?'

'Tell me about the first you met her.'

'You know that. Don't you?'

'No. And I want to hear it from you. In words.'

'Okay…' Aaron smiled, 'I was in the sixth grade of my school. I was a little boy. I was sitting on my desk, it was free track so the classroom was noisy. I was drawing cars on the last page of my note book, I used to do that a lot during my school days.'

'And her?' She was interested.

'Wait…'

'Yeah okay…' She dropped her shoulders.

'I had this bag.' He was explaining a wide imaginary bag to her. 'It was big and heavy. I placed it behind me and when I leaned back it again fell like it had happened a few times before.'

'Okay…'

'And it fell on a girl's foot who was sitting behind me. When I turned to take it from her, she was screaming like "Hey! Aaron Stitch! Your bag always falls on my legs, it hurts me. Keep that in your side." And seven years later she is my girlfriend. My Karuvizhi.'

She laughed at this.

'I was so scared of this girl from then. I won't talk to her until one day.' He shook his finger.

'Oh, what happened that day?'

'Nothing much. She wished me for my birthday with a smile on the corner of her lips.' He froze himself in the memory of that. Each time she wished him for a birthday that smile was there. He just realized it now. 'And that made me fall on a mad crush over her.'

'During the sixth grade?'

He chortled, 'Yes, but the love part is during high school.'

'That's quite a good story, Aaron.'

He smiled, 'At the time I didn't know that after seven years she will be my girlfriend. But the truth is, I don't even know when this infatuation turned into love. It is always her from the beginning. And I don't know why it is always her.'

'Maybe you will come to know someday.'

'Maybe. Hey, do you want to see the gifts I gave her?' Aaron asked and Cara nodded fast with gleaming eyes. He looked deep into them. *No, these are not those eyes.*

'What?'

'Nothing.' Aaron placed Karu's secret box on the bed between them and showed the gifts to Cara. And told her the stories behind them. He showed her selective letters and notes from that box. 'Hey, you have her memory, right?'

'Some of them.'

'So, tell me what's the favourite food of Karu?'

She thought like Karu. 'Favourite food? I don't know. She likes what_'

'Whatever her mom does.' Aaron finished her lines.

'Yes, and also she likes_'

'What my mom does.'

They both broke into laughter, 'Yes. That's it.'

'Phew! This is something that makes her different from any other girl.' Otherwise, she is just a normal girl. She is not my type, you know. She doesn't even know what my job really is. She couldn't understand when I talk to her.' Aaron told Cara without noticing her reactions on these, 'Maybe… Maybe she is not the one I deserve. But still… So what? She doesn't have to be. I will take her as she is. I still love her. And I know it's true.' He turned to look at her. 'What do you say?'

Cara shook her head.

'No, Aaron. You don't know. I told you I sense some memories here. Those powerful memories are not what you know. Those are memories that happened without you. But it was all about you.'

'I don't understand what you are talking about.' He placed the cup on the nightstand beside him. 'Are you okay?'

'Aaron, when I read people's mind I read more than just information. It doesn't look like what people have on their faces and or in their words. The inner mind is different. I can see their secrets, desires, sorrows that hasn't revealed to anyone, some of the emotions they never had perceived. I could literally feel their pain.'

'You don't know how much pain I have felt since I came here. Living in this room is like living in the world of grief. There is another part of Karu only these walls have seen. Most of the nights Karu spent here alone are not good memories.'

'What are you talking about?'

'How can I show you?' She looked around and spotted a pillow. 'Wait…' She took it and placed it on his lap and held his hands into hers to press against the pillow.

Aaron felt a lurch icing his heart. The frigidity squeezed his heart into shards. He was panting and troubled to breathe. The booze went away. Tears slid to his chin and fell on the pillow he was clutching. 'What? What's happening here?'

'This pillow has listened to the unsaid stories of Karu. It has soaked her tears and this pain you are feeling right now, is least as compared to hers.'

'There is an unsent letter written in this pillow. Let me read it for you, "Why? Why Aaron? Why don't you behave like others? Don't you really know the meaning of true love and care? You are showing me these but I'm not the only one for you to love and care for. When was the last time you spoke to your family caringly? Do you know how much your mom and dad crave for your love and caring? Do you know your brother and sister are longing for you to play with them? Earning for them won't fix everything, Aaron. You are not working for them. You are working for yourself. Maybe I might be the whole love of your universe. But Aaron it also has selfishness and when will you realize this? When will you become like others? I want to show you my family as a person who cares and respects people. In what belief I could carry your child, Aaron? Why are you not like others?"'

Aaron's eyes turned cold. He could hardly feel his throat. He took off his hand from the pillow and threw it away. He was still panting. His spine had turned into rubber. He fell on the floor, leaned on the nightstand, and looked at Cara in dread. He didn't want to get harmed by her again.

Cara stood to leave the room. She shook her head, 'I'm sorry to say this, Aaron. But I think you had more than you deserved.'

—— Chapter Sixteen ——

The forest seemed quiet, excluding the chirps of birds, burbs of stream waters, and whirling wind. The sun rays fell straight on her skin, kissing her face, making her hair glow, and failed in revealing the tints hidden in her eyeballs.

Cara was standing alone on the bank of the river. There were no traces of any humans around the place. She undressed. She held her shoulder with the other hand, walking into the shining cold stream water. She walked until she floated. She found herself reflecting on the water. She took her wet hands and brushed on her face. The face and body which she has don't belong to her. She laid flat on the water surface, slowly winging her lean arms.

She observed the sky and the forest. As an observer, many questions raised into her mind. What if she didn't be there? She wondered, how would be the next day. Will the birds still sing the choirs without an audience? Without the presence of an observer will things remain the same here?

She floated, revealing her face and a part of her breasts above the water. She closed her eyes and tried to connect her mind to the species around her. They all connect with the same compound of molecules. That is water. She connected herself to the fishes in the water, hoppers in the grass, frogs on the rocks, birds on the trees. The roots spread in the land connected with each other. Slowly she wandered into the forest and started her interrogating for any traces of recent disturbance in the forest.

Aaron came early in the morning with Cara to the woods. He needed some alone time with Karu. Cara excused herself to wander the woods alone. He had brought a lily flower for Karu in a small vase.

He wore a dark blue T-shirt and black pants and his white sneakers. The starship was not like what it looked like two days before. It had rematerialized itself. The surface of the cubicle was turned into a low light green room. The part of the ship where Karu was, it was warm like a tight hug.

'Are you making this happen? You are imagining your room, right? Whatever...' Aaron was sitting on a stool beside Karu's pod. He could see her breathing. He could feel the nerve on her forehead circulating blood. He wasn't sure about her hearing. He wanted to say many things. They were strong emotions and too alien to him. He tried to put his emotions into words. Karu was quiet. Her eyes were closed.

Then he found what could be the right way to start that. 'Karu, I'm sorry I have made this to you. I have been giving you emotional pain and now physical. I know most of the men won't ask an apology. Or just the men like me. When we say sorry it wouldn't sound like we mean it. But we do. That's all we know. We don't know how to express it.'

'I don't know what to say. But you don't deserve this suffering. I have realized my flaws. I don't know what to do next but I won't do what I did. I promise you, Karu, when you open your eyes, you will be seeing me as a new person.'

Tears hanging in his eyes fell along with his pride. He wiped them and decided to cheer Karu.

'You know what happened yesterday? We are engaged...' Aaron narrated the events that happened on the last day.

It took time to tell her everything and he did it patiently. He did that with patience. He covered every detail. 'You should have been there, Karu. I'm worried that you have missed that day in your life. You should have seen how happy your parents were. I never had imagined these family things would happen. And even if it had, I couldn't guess the moment would be this much beautiful. And you. You must be the most beautiful girl I should have seen yesterday.'

Aaron remembered how Cara was dressed and walked in that aisle. He realised how each moment is important in life. The moments she missed like changing rings and the moments he realised about her like her secret grieving.

'And I felt the pain you had buried in your room. Karu, I know I have been busy lately. I let you in desperation. Today I'm all yours. I have some plans. See what I have brought to you.' Aaron had brought one of Karu's poetry books from her shelf. He read out a poem from the book starting with "She stood as everything."

He kept reading and speaking to her even though he was not sure whether she could hear him or not. Then he played the music from Karu's playlist. The songs she likes, the songs which connect her soul to the memories with Aaron, the songs which she could dedicate only to Aaron. These are songs Aaron never heard and stumbled to pronounce at first. It took time for to Aaron understand the meanings of her songs. When he did it evoked memories from him too. It was another way of saying feelings towards the person we love. Aaron could see her memories, which songs meant to which event in his life. The more he went into them, the more he understood Karu's needs. Some of them said her desires too.

'You, naughty!' He smiled. He came out from his deep thinking. 'These are the songs once you insisted me to listen. I never did. But I like them now. Not because of you. I personally like these meanings. It's soothing and makes me calm.'

For an hour he leaned his face on his palm and kept gazing at her closed eyelids. Then he started speaking, 'You know what, Karu? You were right. I was mean to people. I have never spent my time with family. Even I haven't been kind to you lately. But still, I'm wondering why do people like me anyway? Is that because I'm related to them? After knowing your secret confession, Karu, I don't like myself. Then how do you and others like me?'

He filled his thoughts with many questions that he has never thought of before. He leaned on the pod and looked closely at Karu.

'Still, no one knows me better than you, in fact you know me better than me. You know what I need in my life. And what I need to change in myself. You know all my flaws like no one. Do you know what this means? A person who knows all of a man's flaws and still loves him? She is his wife.'

He got up back, 'You are my wife, Karu. You are.'

A squeaky giggle sounded beside him. He turned to Phrix. It felt awkward for him as he thought no one should hear what he was saying except Karu. 'Why are you laughing at me? You are just a stool. What do you know?' He stretched his feet on the stool. It alarmed.

'And there is another thing I need to tell you. I still don't know why and when I started to love you, but I'm glad that I did. And I do. I love you, Karu. I love you forever until my last breath. I'm dying here while waiting to look into those eyes. If I see them again, I will get the energy to make anything possible in this world. My curse will be gone. I will be healed. I need that hope. So, please, Karu. Please open them for me. Will you? Huh?'

He kept staring at Karu. His mind was playing an illusion of her eyeballs moving. But they weren't. 'Karu, Let's do one thing. I will count to three. You will open your eyes. Okay?'

'One... Two… Three!'

The stool rotated across Aaron hurriedly. Aaron fell to the ground. The stool giggled at him and hovered away from him.

'Hey, you. Stand right there.' He pointed at it.

It levitated away from him. He chased it. It hid behind Karu and played with him for a while. Aaron grabbed it and sat on the top of it pushing himself down. 'Now, what will you do? Huh? Where will you run?'

Phrix moved with Aaron sitting on it. 'Whoa!' It spun from the same place. It stopped for a second. Aaron felt dizzy. Then it spun in the opposite direction. Aaron couldn't hold it anymore. He saw both parts of the ship rotating in front of him. He fell from the stool. 'Okay, you got me.'

Everything looked double to him for a while. He crawled to sit. He spotted his smartwatch on the floor. It didn't look like when he left it. The metal was cold and rusted, the screen was covered with moss and still functioned. He wiped the screen. It was recording audio from the night he left it there. He played that long-duration audio. He skipped to the middle than where the wavelengths showed high.

'Phrix! Where are you?' it was not Cara/Karu's voice.

He sat straight, 'Was there anyone else here?' He asked Phrix.

Phrix's emotions changed. It trembled in fear. 'What happened to you?'

It levitated back under the table.

'Hey, are you scared?' Aaron asked, 'Of whom? Who was this calling you?'

It made sad noises.

'Why are you behaving like this? Did anyone hurt you?'

'Phrix! Can you hear me?' The voice became clear and loud.

'Who was this?' He asked.

'Phrix! Give me a signal. I won't hurt you.' The voice was in a rush, 'I know you are here. I can feel that. Tell me where you are. Open the ship. We shall go home.'

Aaron calmly listened to the voice. It interrogated, 'Where is Cara? Who's with you there?'

Aaron turned to Karu.

'Looks like Cara has got me a present. Wow, I can feel an Earthling prey. She finished my job. Tell Cara I will find her soon. She won't escape from me. I will hunt her down.'

Cara arrived in the doorway in Karu's brown gown. She looked at Aaron who got the traces of the disturbance in this forest before she did.

'Who was that?'

'Aaron, calm down. I will explain.'

'Who was that? And that voice said you have finished her job? What does she mean by prey?'

'She was meaning Karu. Aaron, we need to talk. I should have spoken to you before.'

'I knew this!' he stood up, 'I knew you are that some harmful alien came to destroy mankind. Or at least my life,' he went to Karu and tried to get her out of the pod, 'I'm taking Karu with me. You go somewhere and do whatever you came for. Please let us live in peace.'

'Aaron, you can't take her like this. It won't heal her. Listen to me. She needs another two days to be healed completely. Don't make this more critical!'

'She was like this from the night I put her in. I don't see any wounds healing.' Aaron almost opened the pod.

She held his hands and stopped him from opening, 'Aaron, you have to trust me.'

He threw her hands, 'I don't trust you anymore. Why should I?

'Aaron, listen to me!' She came between him and Karu, 'Let me tell you what really happened. Then you decide yourself whether to trust me or not.'

The world was looking for a big blue moon that night, satellites were busy capturing it's highest quality photos. Nobody or nothing felt suspicious about the floating thing in the atmosphere.

It stood there in the darkness like a secret eye. Observing the spherical land of green, blue and white. The two halves of day and night.

It reflected in Cara's eyes, 'It looks remarkable. Even the dark side.'

'Yes, it does.'

She was there with someone else. Someone of her kind. To add more details, her best friend, Clem who she met after a long time. Their species has no gender classifications, still, they both always chose to be in a female form. They were in a humanoid form of what they took in the previous planet they visited for some information.

The information was more like coordinates. Only Cara could crack the code to find the right passage through the cosmos to reach the place where they were.

'We did it.' Cara was excited.

'No, you did it.' Clem said, joining her to the view.' Your intuition led to this exploration.'

'Look at those lights. It functions all the time. A restless, peaceful world.'

'Also, ignorant.' Clem asked, 'No crystals or metals in this universe are costlier than woods and greens here. And the blue oceans, they are the treasure we cannot steal. Anyway, don't you want to go there for a look?'

'Can we?'

'Yes, we can. That's why we came here all along.'

'I thought our job is just exploration. Are we supposed to wander things there?'

'It's more than that. We need to collect some samples.'

'By samples you meant… Like plants?' Cara asked.

'No, more like a living being.'

'Oh! I see. So, we are going to do the classic movies. Stealing cattle from the sky. Swish!' She motioned like her hands were a spaceship sucking in something from the ground.

Clem chuckled, 'No, Cara, Think of more. Think of big. I just told you this is a field of treasure, will you take just a handful of objects?'

'I don't understand what you are saying.'

Clem leaned on Cara's shoulder from her back. She shared her vision with her, 'Look at them. We need to get one of those most intelligent species on this planet. Those who constructed these buildings, discovered fire and invented wheels. They made history ironically.'

'But why?' Cara was confused.

'There are some gods among us.'

'Gods?'

'They are trying to be. They create evolutions in worlds they own. So, they do research with different species until they can get a new suitable life. Like this!' Clem gestured at the Earth.

'That's gross. Look at them. They are civilized people. Like us. They may have family, unlike us. Doesn't stealing one cause disturbance in the environment? And how do you think they will survive through this interstellar travel?'

'Well, we have a plan. All we need is a female humanoid who is capable of leading an intelligent generation. To survive the innovation should pass through DNA. So, we have to read their mind, find the right one.'

'And for the final process,' Clem gestured at the cryopod. 'This will make our species sleep in hibernation until we land. It will promptly fix any damaged tissues or tumours. Our package will be delivered healthily.'

'This sounds like hell. And what if you have sold one and they would demand more?'

'That's not how it works. One is enough for them. And even if they ask us,' Clem came closer to her with greedy eyes, 'then we will get more job. It's only you and me in this business.'

'Clem, I didn't sign for this. I thought we are explorers.'

'You have never changed… Have you? Look at your life, Cara. You don't have a place to live. You have no one except me. What are you going to do going back to your life empty-handed?'

'That's…'

'Think about what caused you into this situation. This universe is not a kind place to live. We may need to do sins, to fill our stomachs. Did you forget what happened to our place? There is no justice left in the universe. Join me.'

'No, I don't want to be a part of this,' she refused strongly, 'Let's go back.'

'Hey, listen. It's not like you think. You first sit here,' Clem dragged a stool to her. She held her shoulders, 'Remember what I said in the restaurant? I just told you I have done this before. No one is going to get harmed. We are going to take one of them to collect samples. It's a deal either they match with their research or not they will pay us to restore the person we brought. So, we are coming back to drop them here.'

Cara thought of what happened in the restaurant. She was quite compromised. She sat quiet.

Clem said, 'Phrix! Land on the planet resiliently.'

Phrix looked like a stuffed animal pretending to be a pilot. It was connected with the ship. The ship started to move.

Cara became unclear about the restaurant conversation. She felt like it didn't really happen. And she was sure that was not possible to restore. Time and distance don't work that way.

'Wait! Did you induce a fake memory to me?'

'What? Cara stop this. We will talk later.' She ordered Phrix, 'Hey, you. Move faster. We don't have much time.'

Cara understood what Clem was doing. Even if Clem comes back to this place, they cannot be sure how time could turn this journey and the planet. So, it was Clem's only chance to finish this mission. 'You did your cheap scams on me?'

'Phrix!' Cara shouted, 'Stop! Stop this.

Phrix stopped moving.

'What are you doing?' Clem yelled. 'Phrix! Move! Don't listen to her.'

Phrix was confused. It focused on moving the ship again to a part of a forest where there were no lights or any electronic signals.

Cara lifted Phrix in her hands. 'You don't have to do this. Turn back. Let's go home.'

'What are you doing? Don't make me mad. Give him back to me,' Clem tried to take Phrix back from her.

Cara refused and pulled Phrix back. 'I won't let you reach that peaceful land. We have seen the worst. Let them live in peace.'

'What is your problem? I brought you from the tramp. And you behave to me like this? Leave him, Cara.' She pulled Phrix. It cried out in pain and jumped off from both.

They both stared at each other. The floor rotated upward. The ship moved to the ground fast. It had formed into a fireball. The roaring sound screeched the sky. 'This is your fault!'

'What is happening? Phrix, stop this.' Cara lifted Phrix again.

'That's it.' Clem pushed herself on her. The floor was slanting and they both fell on each other. Clem accidentally punched Phrix and it got hurt. It was distrusted by Clem and ran away from her.

Clem was stronger than Cara. She grabbed her head. 'You, get out of my ship and never come back in my life.'

She pulled Cara to the door and opened the door. The hot wind blew on Clem's face. She screamed with her eyes closed. Cara used this time. She pushed her from the door and closed it.

Within a second, the ship crashed on the ground furiously. Everything inside was thrown up and settled down at a place like nothing happened there.

A few minutes later, Cara stood up and looked for Phrix. The spaceship was filled with smoke. She could hardly breathe. She opened the door and got out of the ship. She breathed the air. She placed her feet on that land the first time. It wasn't a good memory. The place where she crashed was burning in fire. The ship had turned itself into a big boulder to adapt to its environment.

Cara's eyes met an injured girl lying on the ground. She dragged her aside from the fire. When she looked into her, she saw a face of innocence. She read her mind.

It was the hardest mind Cara ever read. Most of the parts in her memories were closed like a vault. Her mind was too loud to hear the thoughts. Still, in that vast ocean noise, she was screaming a name in her subconscious. The name was Aaron.

Cara felt she was dying. She took her shape. She changed herself into an earthling. Her bones broke into pieces, her skin burnt like fire and her heart shrunk tightly. She lost most of the energy in the transformation. Then her body cooled itself. She could hardly stand up.

After a few minutes, when she stood up, panting before the fire, she heard a scream over the stream. "Karu! Where are you? I'm coming!"

'That was the night I came between you two.' Cara explained to Aaron. He was calmly waiting for her to finish.

'Okay… Can I ask you something? Am I a joke to you?'

'Aaron! I didn't want to involve you in this. But now I need your help.'

'What? Do I look like a 10-year-old kid who would believe you when you said "I need your help."?'

'Aaron, believe me. We are in a critical situation. If Clem gets this starship, she will take Karu with her. And the consequences are not good.'

'WHY? Why should she take Karu?' Aaron screamed.

'That's because she had sensed Karu's presence here. In some markets, she could make a fortune by selling an intelligent species. Not all of you have that quality. But Karu is one of them.'

Aaron shook his head with a sympathetic smile, 'No, Karu is not an intelligent person like you said. She was a regular girl, who wanted to be a regular housewife in her regular life.'

'So, who is the intelligent person you know? Your friend Destiny?' She tied her arms, 'Aaron, seeing through a telescope and naming all the stars in the sky alone doesn't make one intelligent. See how matured Karu is. She has a visionary thinking mind that is 10 years elder than her. Even housewives are intellectuals. They need to make the home, care for children, and maintain households and bills. They have more intelligence, more intuition, and more responsibility than you ever thought. What Clem wants now is a mother. And Karu is the right one.'

Aaron was confused about what he estimated about Karu. But now he wished he could be right, 'Oh crap! You put Karu in danger! D-A-N-G-E-R, danger.' He threw his hands in the air.

'I know Aaron, I feel sorry for what I did. I didn't have any choice. I tried to save Karu. It was the only way.' She stepped before Aaron. 'But I promise you. Whatever happens to me, I will return Karu as she was to you.'

Aaron couldn't say anything. He just shut his head as if it is going to blow up. He believed her. Still couldn't accept these things happening in this life. No one could advise him to accept reality. These things will not be happening in reality. He couldn't see what will going to happen.

'Now, please give me a day. I will find Clem and deal with her.'

He released his head, 'It's been three days you are here. What did you do? What was your plan then?'

'I don't have a plan. I need to confront her. I cannot leave this planet by leaving a person like her.'

'Then what were you doing? Why did you take time to say all these?' He yelled at her.

'Because I was busy living your girlfriend's life!' She yelled back, 'At first, I was grateful to have a family like this.' She outburst, 'Then I was sick. Everyone in that house keeps judging me for whatever I do. They keep calling me if I take time in the bathroom. Karu's mother keeps asking me why I'm late in my menstruation cycle. Tell me, Aaron. What should I answer her?'

Aaron stood answerless. Then he got one. 'You can fake it.'

She sighed, 'Agrhh! Aaron, please get me out of that house. I will find Clem and confront her. Then you take Karu and live your happy life with her. Let's make another deal here.'

—— Chapter Eighteen ——

Aaron was waiting in his car outside Karu's house. Now he doesn't need to wait on the corner of the street. He has all the rights to visit the house.

'It's strange.'

'What is strange?' Aaron asked Edward in his school uniform in the backseat.

'You picked us up from school. Asking our help to lie to both the parents so that you may get Karu to stay in our house. And you agreed to go to the Pizzeria with us.'

'I told you, we need to go to an important place tomorrow. Her parents won't allow us. And also, it would be a good time for us to bond with Karu.'

'She's been coming to our house for like 5 years.' Edward leaned on the front seat, 'Tell me the truth, Aaron. Are you two going to see a new house? You won't live with us after marriage, right?'

'What? Why are you thinking that? That's not true.'

'Hmmm...' He went back, 'It would be good actually. I may get your room. I'm sick about living with Stella.'

Aaron didn't reply to anything. Because Stella was his saviour then. Stella has this superpower to speak in a sweet manner. She could convince anyone. So, to get Cara free from Karu's house, Aaron chose to ask for Stella's help. Stella had to lie to Karu's parents that she has a mathematics exam on Monday. And she had to convince them to send Karu to tutor her and Ed. For this, Aaron had to bribe Stella and the only witness, Edward, with pizzas.

After ten minutes, Stella in her school uniform came out with Cara. Karu's mother came with a whole branch of red bananas. She placed it on the backseat and Stella sat beside it. Cara opened the door and sat on the front seat. She had a bag of her clothes for the next three days and a box of colostrum puddings in her hand.

'Remember what I said. Be nice to your in-laws. Don't be careless. Take your own responsibilities.' Her mother pointed out the qualities of a good daughter-in-law. Aaron understood how it would be hard to be in that house for Cara. And for Karu.

'I know, Maa!' Cara sighed, 'You have said that a thousand times.'

Aaron noticed her. Even her eyelashes were acting as Karu. Same as how Karu would speak with her mother. *Who is she? How can an explorer have this much talent?*

'We shall go.' She told him. Aaron greeted her mother and started the engine. He wanted to go from there before Karan comes.

When they crossed the street, Edward leaned forward, 'So! Pizzeria?'

'Why are you so eager to go there?' Aaron asked.

'I will say!' Stella leaned forward on Cara's seat. 'Ed's new girlfriend works there. And she doesn't believe his brother owns a Mustang.'

'Darla, calm down. The kids are with Aaron.'

'They are lying. Don't you see?' Aaron's mother was walking in the hall, 'When is the last time Aaron picked up the kids?'

'Well, it will be today. What is the date today actually?' Aaron's dad checked the calendar, 'April 21.'

The door thudded. Stella and Edward rushed inside. 'Mom! Dad!'

'Kids! Where did you go?'

'I told you Aaron picked us up. We went to pick up Karu and then to have Pizza.' Ed explained.

Stella made an evil smile. 'And guess who we met at the Pizzeria!'

'Shut up!' Edward glared at her. 'We bought you cakes, Mom.'

Cara walked inside the house for the first time. Aaron had gone to park his car. Aaron's mother noticed the bag on her shoulder.

'Karu! What is happening here?' Mom looked confused.

'Nothing. I just wanted to spend some time with you guys. Anything wrong with that?'

'No, nothing is wrong. Did Aaron pick up kids and you all hang out today?'

'Yes, we did.'

'Ha!' She was surprised, 'This usually won't happen.'

'I think it will happen hereafter.' She shrugged.

'Because of my new daughter-in-law.' Aaron's father ushered her to walk inside.

That night, after dinner, they all came in nightdresses to sit on the floor of the hall to play a board game Edward brought.

'This game is called "The imposter."' Ed took out a board with a map of a starship and little coins of space travellers.

'What is this about?' Stella asked.

The whole family gathered in a circle around the board. Aaron and Cara sat against each other. Edward and Stella on one side and his mother and father on the other.

'Let me explain,' Ed took the coins and card from the box and arranged them, 'We all are on an interstellar journey in a spaceship. Mysteriously, an alien has come into our ship and took the place of any one of us. So, one of us is an alien. An imposter.'

Aaron's eyes met Cara's.

'Sounds boring.' Stella said.

'Shut up until I finish the explanation.' He took a dice and rolled it on the board. 'See, to start the game, we need to get 6 in the dice.'

'We should split into two teams. Red and Blue. Let the boys be blue and girls are red.' He placed a coin on the starting point, 'When you come to the entrance, you should take a card from this deck.' He took the deck of cards, 'There are cards which say your roles in the ship. Like Pilot, General, Engineer, Janitor, Inspector, and the Imposter.'

'Whoever gets the imposter is the alien.'

'And the Inspector needs to find who the imposter is?' Cara asked Ed.

'You are right, Karu!'

Aaron felt suspicious, 'How do you know? Is this a universal game?' No one got what he meant by universal.

'No, we will play a game like this called "King and Queen" Cara told Aaron what she gathered from Karu's memory, 'There will be five sheets. King, Queen, Minister, Police, and Thief. Police have to guess the thief.'

'Yes, in this whoever gets the inspector can guess who the imposter is. If the inspector finds the imposter, then the first team that reaches the endpoint is the winner. If he guesses it wrong, the player will be dismissed from the game and then whoever gets the Inspector card again can guess it again.'

'Alright, let's start the game.' Aaron's mother said. 'It's getting late.'

After 15 minutes, the dice was rotating from hand to hand and it kept rolling on the board. The coins kept moving. The cards kept shuffling.

Aaron and Cara were moving at the same speed. They had reached 75% of the game.

Aaron's mother was stuck in 20% while his father reached 60%.

Edward reached the endpoint fast. And waiting for his team members to arrive. His card was the pilot.

Stella reached 90%. She wanted to defeat Aaron. So, she used her card. 'I'm the inspector. And I suspect Aaron is the imposter here.'

'Why me?' Aaron asked.

'I know it's you. You have a bad poker face, Aaron.'

Stella was almost right. He was the imposter. But he had switched the card already. Then he was the Engineer.

'Okay, then see it yourself.' He showed the card.

'Yeh! Stella is out of the game!' Edward cheered up. Stella's coin was out. His mom was away from the endpoint. Only Cara was his competitor from the red team.

'Alright, let's move.' Cara said.

After 20 minutes, Cara and Aaron reached 90%. Surprisingly, Aaron's father moved to 95%. His mom was in 30%.

'Come on, dad one more 6. You will enter the endpoint!' Edward guided him.

'It's my turn.' Cara protested.

'Oh, I'm sorry, dear. Here you go.' Aaron's father handed her the dice.

'Wait!' Aaron stopped the game. 'I'm the inspector now!' He had noticed Cara taking his imposter card from him and waited for the moment to strike her coin.

'Okay, what's your problem Inspector?' Cara asked. 'You sound so serious.'

Everyone laughed at him.

'I know you are the imposter.'

'How do you know?'

'I just know,' He shrugged, 'You look like some alien who took Karu's place and pretends to be her.'

She smiled, 'Are you sure?'

'One hundred percent_' Aaron looked at the card she was showing.

'See, I'm just a janitor.' She made pitiful faces.

'Aww! How could you suspect innocent Karu?' Stella asked. 'Poor Aaron is out of the game now.'

'How did this happen?'

'Dad, it's only you. We are in two vs two. Roll the dice.' Ed threw him the dice.

'Sure, son, look at the game now.' He rolled and it was a six. He moved to the endpoint.

'Whoohoo! We won!' Edward's face brightened.

'No, I won.' Howard revealed his card. 'I'm the imposter!'

Aaron yelled. 'What?'

'Dad!' Edward was shocked.

'Howard? Well played,' she nodded at him proudly. 'Okay, kids. Let's call it a night.' Aaron's mother stood up and commanded them to wrap up. 'Stella, take Karu to your room.'

Aaron yawned in tiredness.

'Ed, you take your bed sheets and sleep with Aaron tonight.'

'Okay!' He rushed to take his bedsheets.

'What? Why my room?' Aaron asked. No one replied to him. Everyone went to their room.

After a minute, Ed came into his room. He locked the door and took out hidden PC game DVDs from the bedsheet. 'Huh? What do you say? Shall we play?'

'No,' Aaron chuckled.

'Please Aaron!'

'I will tell mom. Go to sleep.'

'But, Aaron, when we played games last time it was joysticks connected with television. A lot of things have changed now.'

Aaron got a nostalgic memory of playing games with his brother in that classic video game set. *How did a small green chip hold a lot of fun time, back then? Now in the air, tons of data are transferring.*

'Alright, but just one game,' he applied this condition seriously, 'I will sleep early.'

It was 3 AM when they won the battleground.

—— Chapter Nineteen ——

Aaron and Cara drove to the woods and they entered the starship. Aaron changed the flowers in the vase. He brought sunflowers. He thought the sunflowers would make Karu smile when she wakes up.

Cara took what she wanted to pick up from the ship. She took a glance at Aaron. The way he was looking at Karu. His tight jawline was telling how worried he was to see her like this. Cara wanted to know how he was going through. But she had promised him to not read his mind. Aaron's mind is not as complex as Karu's. But everyone misread it at first. Cara never thought there is another part of him caring this much about his girl.

Aaron was attracted more to Destiny. But it was an undiscovered connection. He couldn't do it until he was with Karu. That's why he wished Karu shouldn't be his girlfriend. But in his mind they both were different. And he was feeling guilty for it. Surely, no one else could replace Karu in his heart, mind and soul. And also he was helping Cara in her venture.

Aaron turned to Cara and found her staring at him. 'What?'

'Shall we go?' Cara asked.

'Where?'

'I don't know. But I know the way.'

It was not exactly the right way. She kept telling him the direction and Aaron kept driving there.

'This direction!' her hand moved quickly here and there like she was having Alien Hand Syndrome.

Alien Hand Syndrome. Aaron chortled at this thought.

'What?' She asked.

'Nothing,' he smiled and decided to have a conversation, 'So, what was your life before. Before you came here.'

She nodded with a smile on her face, 'At last, Aaron Stitch cares about what I was. Or just now you got the thought that I too had a life out there?'

'You know I'm not into chit chats.'

'Okay, I don't have a family. My place was destroyed in famine. So, no background. And I'm an actor.'

Aaron found it weird, 'Actor in?'

'Various planets. Just like your planet, there are many filmmakers out in the universe. I was once a stage actor. Then I went for auditions to get a role in the movies for the last 2 years. They are small years. Like 200 days with 18 hours per day.' She changed direction.

Aaron turned and drove on a highway, 'Okay, so, what happened then? Did you get any part?'

'The only part I got was some lame joke show that only broadcasts on the screens of restaurants. Only travellers or explorers will watch it.' She signalled him to go forward.

'You can make it good. Improvise on what you had.'

'I was not supposed to. I had to act stupid to make the diners spurt their drink so that they order more.'

'I will give you a tip to act like a stupid. You should watch the movies made here.'

'Yeah, I have. I have watched 756 movies so far.'

'How?' He turned to her, 'When did you watch all these?'

'While reading memories from people. If I get extra time, I read movies and stories they have seen or read.'

'Oh, that's new.' He decelerated the car to listen to her clearly.

'Yes, and you know what? You and Karan share some common movie interests. Maybe a movie night can help both of you to bond well.'

He sighed, 'Ahh… I don't think we are ready for that.'

She laughed.

Aaron wanted to ask Cara questions. 'And… She is your friend? The other person?'

'Hmmm? Very well, yes.' She turned to the window. 'The only person I have close to a family.'

'You got betrayed.'

'No, it's different. I sabotaged her mission. I knew she had her risks. It's not easy to come this far. I felt it was the right thing to do. She might be mad at me. She will try to kill me anytime. No doubts about that.' She turned back to him.

He nodded, 'That's what I was thinking. Shall I ask you something?'

'What?'

'What would you do if you get to meet her?'

'I will try to speak to her and try to convince her to go back without harming anyone.'

'But you did that last time.'

'Yes.' Cara nodded.

'You both had a fight then.'

'Yes of course. We had. So what?'

'Nothing.' He shook, 'Just I wanted to know.'

'You are expecting to see us fight. Aren't you?' she asked.

'No, I don't. Why should I even think that?' He waved, 'I hope you both get together and reach to the place where you came from for world peace.'

Cara smiled and turned to the window. 'This way!'

It is a good thing she has promised me that she won't read my memory. Isn't it cool to watch two aliens fighting each other? Well, not if one of them looks like your girlfriend. But still, I'm curious.

'Stop, stop right here,' Cara pointed her right hand at a vintage building. 'There! She must be there.'

'We can't go in there. We don't know whose place this is.' Aaron studied the place. 'It looks like a party hall.'

'Just drive inside. I will make an excuse.'

Aaron tightened his lip and drove into the archway. There was a low slope after the gate. He drove slowly. The security in the gate didn't find them doubtful as the car looked expensive.

Aaron pulled over, got out of the car and looked around the place. He was surprised to see the SYS logo in the banner there. It said "Welcome to the 10th Anniversary Celebration"

'It's my office event. What are we doing here?' He asked her.

'May I park your car, Sir?' a valet came along to ask for his car's key politely.

Aaron handed him the key, 'Please handle it with care.'

'I will take care, Sir. You have a nice day.' He nodded, 'Have a nice day, Madam.'

'Oh,' Cara replied, 'Thank you. You too! Have a nice_'

Aaron pulled her arm and asked her, 'What are we doing here?'

'I don't know,' she opened her right palm.

'What the heck is that?' Aaron cried out on seeing one of the iris fish under the skin of her palm. It was merged into her. He didn't like to see that. Karu's sunrise was alienated.

'This will find Clem. It belongs to her.' The eyeball rotated like a compass.

'Well, then, ask it. Where is she?'

'I don't know what has happened to it. It is not working now.' She bewailed.

He yelled at her, 'What are you speaking? There must be hundreds of guests. Can you recognize her?'

'I think I can. And I'm sure she will be here.'

'Sir, are you invited?' An organiser in a white shirt and red tie wanted to cross-check their names with the list he had.

'I'm a staff. My name is Aaron Stitch.' He replied.

'Aaron!'

Aaron turned to see Damian calling him, 'That's my boss. Behave yourselves,' he whispered to Cara.

'Hello, sir.'

'I know you will come today! But not in a T-shirt.' He checked Aaron's attire which was a dark green T-Shirt, black jeans and casual shoes. 'So, is this the lucky girl who is going to marry you?'

Aaron was embarrassed about the dressing. 'Err… Yes, sir. This is Karu… Karuvizhi.'

Cara had removed Stella's denim jumper she had on. It was a surprise for Aaron. She was dressed in Karu's maroon embroidered tunics and blue pants looking stunning for the party. And she had opened her hair falling straight.

'Karu, I have told you about Damian, right?' Aaron said to Cara. Cara and Damian shook hands.

'Yes, he has told me everything. From the moment he met you on the elevator to the last time you wished for the engagement. Like everything.'

Here we go, again, the drama starts. Aaron rolled his eyes.

'Really? But Aaron has kept you as a secret to everyone here. Let's move inside.'

Damian walked Aaron and Karu into the open lawn area where the event took place. The place was decorated with colour papers and balloons and filled with hundreds of people who were guests and staff. Everyone dressed in party mode. They all held a plate, filling it with food. A woman in her early 30s welcomed them.

'This is my wife, Rachel. She is running a multi-cuisine restaurant in the city. This all food comes from her restaurant,' Damian introduced Cara to his wife, 'Aaron's fiancée, Karu.'

Cara shook her hand. She read her mind. Rachel had a strong passion for business in her mind. But her husband was handling most of the things. She was craving recognition. A simple appreciation, maybe.

Cara knew how to give it to her. 'Aaron has mentioned about you too. He loves your cooking. The potato wedges he ate a long time ago in your house, he still speaks about it.

He always says women should be more of an organizer like you.'

'Oh, that's so sweet of you, Aaron,' her heart melted in Cara's words. She smirked at him.

Aaron, who didn't even remember what he ate that day smiled back. 'That's nothing.'

'You take care of Aaron. I will introduce Karu to others.' Damian left Aaron with Rachel and ushered Cara to the office staff.

Cara met Sprayman, Dark chocolate, Robot pants, and many others. She read their memories and regretted it.

Rachel was so happy that Aaron had mentioned her to Karu. She filled Aaron's plate with lots of dishes.

'Thank you. I think I've had enough of this.' Aaron lifted his plate and walked behind her.

'Shoot! Don't say anything. Taste everything around here.' In a few minutes the plate had added more weight.

Damian came to Aaron. He looked surprised. 'Aaron, how many languages does Karu speak?'

Aaron checked what Cara was doing. Cara was speaking to foreign clients in their language.

'Well, sir… We truly don't know what she is capable of.' He chewed his food.

Cara read each one of the office employees. She tried to classify them into teams. But she couldn't. Many of them had two or more faces. Nancy smiled at her friendly. Cara read her mind thinking, *'Oh! Where did that bitch Destiny go? I can't wait to see this girl burning her face.'*

'Glad to see you too,' she smirked at Cara.

'Hello, miss. I heard that you are Aaron's fiancée,' a middle-aged man offered his hand to her, she held his hand, 'I'm Nazir.'

'Oh, Aaron has told me about you.'

'Did he say anything good?'

'Yes, many good things.' She went through his memories of Aaron. She felt frustration in him. A disappointment. Rage on the management and a little on Aaron. Then she found out how he stole Aaron's idea and was going to present it to the foreign clients that day. He didn't even feel regret about that.

'Then, good. I have to prepare for a meeting. We will meet again.' He smiled and left the place.

Cara walked to sit beside Aaron. He was eating a load of food on his tyre-sized plate. 'Hey, didn't you eat anything?'

'Aaron, what is wrong with this place?'

He gulped the food. 'What happened?'

'People around here. They hate each other and still pretend like they are not.'

'Oh, that's the fun of being in a workplace.' He took one of his four soft drinks Rachel offered, 'Please don't spoil it with your drama.'

'Why did you let Nazir take your idea?'

'You got that? Okay… That idea is for the company. What is wrong with someone else saying it out? I don't care if they take my idea. I can come up with another one.' He took her fork and pointed before Cara. 'But I feel pity for those who cannot.'

Cara felt a little compromised by speaking to him. 'Hmmm... This is the first time I have misunderstood a person.'

'Are you talking about me?' He smiled.

'Yes,' she nodded, 'You are not like I estimated. You are a kind caretaker and at the same time a person living with ethics. You are a good human, Aaron.'

'Well, it's good to hear from someone from outside!'

'Aaron, the meeting is going to start.' Damian arrived at the table with a brown overcoat in his arms. 'Here, wear this over.'

'Okay, sir.' He stood up.

'Damian! Let him eat.' Rachel scowled at him.

'Okay! I'm sorry. Aaron, finish your food and meet me at the conference room.' He turned to Cara, 'Karu, why don't you join us?'

'Me?'

'You would be helpful to handle our clients,' he brought Cara with him to the Conference hall.

In the elevator, Cara asked, 'Mr. Damian, shall I say something that Aaron has been worried about for long?'

'What is that?'

'He feels bad for his senior... What's his name?' Cara was performing the plot she made.

'Nazir?'

'Yes, him'

'What's wrong with Nazir? Is he troubling Aaron?' Damian seemed serious.

'No, no, not like that. Aaron feels he should be governed. After all, he is his first mentor who made him come to this position. Even many times he said, Nazir should be in his position.'

'Oh, I don't know Aaron has this thought in him. Actually, he is right.' Damian thought deep. 'Okay, Karu. I will take care of this. Don't worry. Thanks for reporting this to me.' He smiled, 'With you, we are understanding Aaron more.'

She smiled back. The elevator belled and opened.

The party hall had a conference room bigger than they have in the office. The foreign clients were sitting in the front row and Damian gave an introduction to the company and broadcasted a few videos of previous events and achievements.

Aaron and Cara sat in the second row. Cara asked him, 'He prominently wants them to invest in the company. Doesn't he?'

He replied, 'If Damian makes a talk with you, please don't join our company.' Cara giggled.

Damian finished his speech, 'Gentlemen, excuse me to make an announcement here. It's a big decision I made in a very short time. And I'm a hundred percent sure that I'm right about that.'

'This is new.' Aaron felt something weird.

'Nazir, can you come forward?' He called out and Nazir walked on the stage to present Aaron's presentation.

'Ladies and Gentlemen. Meet, Mr. Nazir,' He talked like introducing Nazir to the office team too, 'Our new General Manager of SYS.'

Everyone went in shock including Nazir.

'Let's give your hands!' Damian asked for claps and the room applauded for Nazir. He turned to the foreign clients, 'Gentleman, Nazir will take care from here. He had something to present to you.'

Nazir was surprised about his sudden promotion. The general manager of the whole company. Above all of the departments. Nazir felt that was big for him. More than he wanted. He felt a sudden guilt for taking Aaron's presentation.

'Gentleman, let me present you…' He decided not to do that, 'Aaron on the stage.'

'Why me?' Aaron was confused. Damian signalled him to go forward. He joined with Nazir.

'This is Aaron Stitch, the creative head of the Advertising department. I'm so proud to say that I'm his trainer.' He placed his arm on Aaron's shoulder. 'Aaron has prepared a wonderful presentation that will make you clear all the queries you have about the marketing approach. He will present it now.'

'Go ahead, Aaron.' Nazir told him and went to stand beside Damian. Damian was happy to see that event.

Aaron didn't hesitate for a moment. He started his presentation. He spoke charmingly. He kept the attention of the audience.

Nazir gladly pleased Damian for his promotion. 'Thank you, Damian. I don't know if I deserve this. But I will do my best.'

'I know you will, Mr. Nazir. And if you want to thank, you need to thank Aaron and Karu. She told me Aaron's opinion about you should be governed.'

Aaron looked at Nazir in the middle of his speech. Nazir seemed to be drenched in emotion. *Right. It's one of her dramas. I told her not to do anything. Anyway, I can use this moment to fill emotions with my words. Can't I?*

'That's the end of the presentation, gentlemen. Now I need to speak to you personally. I recommend you to invest in our company. Because we are more than a company, a family. You might have heard this from any company in the world. But I'm saying this as the pet child of this family. We build things together. And the bond between us. So, if you have already decided to join us, welcome to our family.'

— Chapter Twenty —

Everyone felt sleepy after eating too much. It was just staff. Guests took off after the event. While they staff were waiting for the dessert, Damian and Rachel entertained them with fun games. They called out each person to choose tasks written in the papers from a bowl. And then they insisted on them to do it. They both were very happy about signing with foreign clients.

Aaron stayed away from the crowd to avoid the games. He walked to Cara and asked her, 'What do you think you are doing?'

'What?' She asked.

'The drama you are doing here. You don't have to do these. What are you? My guardian angel?'

She smiled, 'You can take it in that way. Are you happy now?'

'Me? Look at my colleagues,' he pointed at the sleepy heads. 'Do they look happy?'

Cara thought they were sad. 'I don't think so. Why? Did I do something wrong?'

'Yes, you did.' Aaron sounded serious. 'You gave the company to the Nazi Army. Soon we all will be terminated.'

'I'm sorry, I don't understand this whole office system.' She looked scared.

He laughed. 'I was just kidding.' He winked at her.

She stared at him and it turned into a smile. A smile on the corner of her lips.

That's the smile of Karu. He wanted a distraction. Then it alarmed him why they both came here in the first place. 'Alright, what happened to the reason we came here?'

'It's not working,' she showed her palm, 'I think it needs energy. I have to eat.'

'Well, look around you. You are at a food court,' Aaron ushered her to a table and took a plate of meatloaf, and gave it to her.

'Eww! No meat. I want *Idli*.'

'Don't behave like a child. Eat something from here.'

'Aaron! Why are you scolding Karu?' Nazir showed up there. 'Come on, sweetheart, I will show you where *Idli* is.'

'Thank you!' Cara smiled and followed him. Aaron was left alone. He looked around and spotted an open bar.

Nazir brought her to the food buffet and filled her plate. Cara was glad for his kindness, 'Thank you! I think I'm enough of these.'

'I think you won't. Wait, Karu, I will get you a fork.'

'No, thank you. I like to eat with hands.' She started eating as Karan taught her.

'Excuse me,' a voice came between them. It was Clem. She walked out as she was too irritated on the games happening inside.

Nazir was blocking her way, 'Oh, look who's here…' he made a surprised look on Clem. 'Have you met Aaron's fiancée?'

Cara was holding the plate in her one hand and her other hand had food, 'Don't take me wrong. I can't shake your hands.' She glimmered, 'I'm Karu.'

'Hi, I'm Destiny.'

Cara lifted her face and looked at her. A pair of mysteriously distracted eyes was incompatible to the warm smiling lips. 'Oh, it's you! I have heard a lot about you.'

'Really? He has told you about Destiny too?' Nazir asked. 'We never thought Aaron would be this much open to anyone.'

'I'm so happy for both of you. Now please excuse me, I'm going for a drink.' Clem passed across them.

'Nice meeting you!' Cara focused back on the food.

Clem was wearing a white sleeve with wavy flocks and black pants. Her hair was straight. She was tired of pretending to be nice to people. She spotted Aaron sitting on the open bar. She walked to the bar set up with bamboo walls.

A bartender in a red polo shirt greeted Aaron. 'Shall I make you a drink, sir?'

'Can I get a glass of bourbon?' Aaron asked.

'Sure, sir. Shall I put some ice?' He poured the drink in a glass.

'Yeah, sure.'

'Here you enjoy your drink, sir.' The bartender placed the drink.

Clem sat on the long stool beside Aaron. 'I will have the same.'

Aaron noticed her. He felt an awkward happiness on her arrival. 'Hey! Des.'

'Aaron, how was your engagement?' She took and sipped her drink.

'Yeah, it went very well. Do you want to see Karu?' He pointed at Cara. 'She's there, eating.'

Cara was tasting a red spherical and sugar-coated sweet. She liked it much. 'What is this?'

The server answered, 'Honey candies, Ma'am.'

'I love it! Give me more!'

Clem looked grumpy. 'She looks nice. I'm happy for you.'

'So, what are you up to?'

'Nothing.' She said with a straight-face.

'Okay…' Aaron thought about what to say. *What could I say? I feel like there is nothing between us two. What happened? Suddenly one of the important people in my life has become an acquaintance.*

'See… Des, I don't know what is going on between us. But I felt guilty. I don't know why. We were good friends. And I want to be all the time.'

Clem chuckled, 'Friends. I lost the gravity in this word. But I feel good with you. Let me give you an advice, Aaron. Don't feel guilt for anything you did. No one is good enough to feel for.'

Aaron zipped his lips for a while. He finished his drink in silence. He couldn't say more. He thought she meant the friendship was over. Then he felt guilt again for something he did earlier. 'Hey, that day you asked about a pendant. Is that important?'

She shook, 'Not like that.' Then she nodded, 'Actually, it is. It was my grandfather's. I always had it on my desk since I was in school hostel and it suddenly disappeared. That's why I asked.'

'Well, I'm sorry.' He shrugged.

She finished her drink, 'Why?'

'I took it that day. And I'm terribly sorry, I lost it somewhere.'

'Where did you lose it, Aaron?' she sounded serious.

'Ah…That's the problem. I don't know.'

'Tell me!' Clem pulled him close, 'Did you go to any forest that night?' She grasped his arms and held them for a while. She read his memory. She saw everything. From the crash happened in that night, the cryopod, the engagement, and the reason why he came there for.

'Yes, how do you know?' he asked and didn't get any answers. *What is wrong with her?*

'Where is she?' Clem spotted Cara. She jumped from the stool and marched to Cara.

'Who?' Aaron was puzzled.

Cara who had just finished eating wiped her mouth with a tissue and looked at her palm. The creature in her palm had awakened. It showed directly at Clem walking to her in the skin of Destiny.

Aaron couldn't understand what was happening. He kept looking at them. But Cara understood everything. She tightened her jaws and clenched her fist.

Clem tackled her without any warning. She punched her in the face two times, 'You pushed me out of my own ship!' She shrieked and punched her again.

Cara pulled her down and punched back as hard as she could. Aaron rushed to them and pulled Cara from her back, 'What are you doing? Why are you hurting Destiny?'

She pushed him back, 'That is not Destiny. It's Clem!'

Aaron felt fiery on the skin behind his ears. He checked at Destiny. She didn't look like Destiny anymore to him. *It's another alien. Clem!*

Clem stood up with vengeance in her eyes. She ran to Cara, choked her neck, and slammed her on a table. She tried to strangle her to death. Cara's hand met a ceramic plate. She smashed it on Clem's face. She kicked Clem and jumped on her on the floor.

Everyone there gathered at the place. 'Oh my god! They are fighting!'

'What should we do?' Sparyman was freaked out. 'Shall we call an ambulance?'

'They don't seem to be injured.' Nancy said, 'Let's see what happens.'

For Aaron, he got what he wanted which was witnessing two aliens fighting each other. But for the other pairs of eyes around there, it looked like Karu and Destiny were are fighting for Aaron.

Nazir shouted 'Aaron! Do something!'

'What?'

'Your both girlfriends are hurting each other.' Nazir yelled at him in shock. 'Stop them!'

'These are not my girlfriends!' he screamed. He stood there like he had nothing to do with them.

Cara and Clem were fighting fast. They threw on each other whatever was nearby. Clem twisted Cara's hand and locked her in a submissive position for a moment.

Then she released her. Cara fell. They both were panting and staring at each other. They didn't look like friends.

Damian arrived at the place. 'Okay, guys, everyone should go inside. Desserts are waiting for you. Come on! Leave them alone.' He ushered all of them into the party hall.

'I knew that bitch would do something like this.' Someone from the crowd has started gossiping.

Damian touched Aaron's shoulder, 'Aaron! You know my mentor, he once said, "Never get into a chick's fight." So, take care of yourself.' He patted him and left the place.

Clem smiled at Cara. She ran from the place. Cara got up and chased her. Aaron had no idea what was happening and what he should do. He followed them to the Hall entrance.

He came to the parking lot and searched for Cara and Clem. A red car in high-speed came towards him. Cara pushed him on the grass to save his life. The car thrusted past from the gate.

Cara shouted, 'She is escaping. We need to catch her.'

She rushed to the car parking, 'Give me the keys!' She screamed at the valet. He politely gave her the keys like nothing strangely happened there.

Cara opened Aaron's car and sat on the driver's seat. Aaron followed her. 'What? Are you driving the car now?'

She started the engine and scowled at him, 'Are you coming or not?'

Aaron rushed to the passenger seat and closed the door. The car rose at a high speed. It flew through the high slope before the gate and drifted on the road. Cara spotted Clem's car that she had stolen from the parking lot. She drove fast to catch her.

She honked at the traffic cars and tried to pass them as fast as she could. She sped enough to catch Clem's car. Aaron from the passenger seat was freaked out about the things happening.

Cara was stuck between the cars moving around her. She continued to honk, pushed the brakes and took left and right turns to escape from stumbling.

For Aaron, he couldn't observe things happening around him. His vision was blurred. He just heard the honks, gas, brakes, other driver's scolding, and gas again. Then the engine roared. Aaron was thrown up and down. Then he managed to wear the seat belt.

Clem had sped away from them. Cara finally managed to get out of the traffic. She changed the gears and hit the gas to raise forward. For a few minutes, she forgot there was a brake system in this car. She sprinted towards the red car. She reached alongside Clem. There came a bridge before them.

Aaron met Clem in the shape of Destiny. She shrieked at him and rotated the steering suddenly at them.

Cara moved aside while Clem's car flew over the bridge. Cara screamed from under the bridge, 'Oh, Come on!'

She accelerated towards the end of the bridge. Aaron headed out and spotted the red car. It had reached the end while they were halfway through.

Then they had been chasing Clem for like half an hour. The sky got dark. They had reached a suburban area. They crossed farms and fields. Now they were driving on a narrow road between cornfields.

Cara finally spotted Clem's car. She raced against time. She reached 10 feet away from Clem. Aaron was tired on this ride. He felt his head was spinning. And what he ate at the festival was jumping up and down inside his stomach.

He opened the window to get some air. The dust of corn crops from the wind tore his face at that high speed. He could hardly open his eyes. He checked Clem's car.

Clem turned towards the cornfields.

'She turned!' Aaron screamed, 'Right!'

'Got it.' Cara drifted and turned her path into the cornfield. The tyres were smoking. In the middle of cornfields, both the cars smashed the corps and drove through it.

Cara couldn't see where she was going. She followed the roar of the engine. A scarecrow fell on the car's deck. Aaron screamed. His heartbeat went high.

'Don't scream!' Cara hushed him.

They couldn't hear the sound of the other car. They found the car stopped in the middle of the field. Cara stopped the car and stepped out of it and she checked for Clem.

But there was no one inside it. She stood on the roof of the red car and took an eagle view of the corn field, but Clem was nowhere to be seen. "Damn! Where did she go?" Cara baffled.

Aaron couldn't digest what just happened. He had already come out of the car and threw up everything he ate earlier. He felt a little relieved after vomiting. But still, his head was spinning. He couldn't stand straight. He leaned on his car.

'Ughrrr! Where did she go?' Cara stumped the roof of the car and jumped on the crown.

'What the hell is happening here?' He cried out.

'I don't have any explanation, Aaron. I don't know how this happened.' Cara sounded worried.

'If this isn't Destiny, then, where is she?' He yelled.

163

'I don't know. But the situation is getting life-threatening.'

'What?' Aaron screamed. He couldn't perceive her words.

'She had read my memories. She knows, Aaron!' She cried out, 'She knows where the starship is. She will reach there, anytime.'

That quaked Aaron's mind, 'What? Then what about Karu? She is not safe there.' He freaked out.

'I know. We have to do something now.' She calmed herself.

'Let's go there.'

'No,' she tried to calm him. 'I will take this car and go to the starship. I will protect Karu. You go and check about Destiny. Then come to the ship.'

'Alright.' He nodded. They both got into the cars. Before starting the engine, Aaron thought about switching places. *I should be with Karu.*

But he felt Karu would be safer with Cara. He started the car and drove to Destiny's apartment.

—— Chapter Twenty-One ——

Aaron took a long drive from the fields and reached Elysian City as fast as he could. It was around 8 PM when he reached Destiny's Apartment.

Why am I getting feelings for Destiny again? What is this? I know I'm engaged to Karu. But I care about Des. And how can I not be guilty about that? I don't feel wrong about that. Right now, there is only question popping in my mind. How did she get involved in this? I want to make sure if she's okay.

He parked his car in front of the building and rushed to the stairs. He rushed across a middle-aged lady, Destiny's neighbour and pushed the basket of clips she was holding. He rushed back and helped her to pick them up, apologized, and then he rushed to Destiny's apartment.

He stopped at her door. He was scared to see what could be at the other side of the door. Clenching his fist with no idea of what would be there behind the door, he knocked.

The door opened. 'Aaron?'

'Des?' Aaron was confused to see her there. And he felt a little relieved and pleased about it.

He alarmed, 'Des! Are you alright?'

'Yes, I'm alright. Have you come to check on me?' She opened the door fully and gestured him to get in. She was wearing a navy blue sleeveless shirt and black jeans.

'Yes, what happened to your phone?' he walked in, 'I have been trying to call you this whole week. Anyway, I need to talk to you about something serious.'

'Relax Aaron.' she closed the door and followed him, 'I think I need to talk to you too.'

'Seriously, what were you doing here? I tried to call you_' She opened the bedroom door. Aaron went thunderstruck on seeing Destiny sleeping in her bedroom in a Grey silk night suit.

He stood speechless. He looked at the person who opened the door for him. Again he had to witness this dual illusion in reality.

'I know you will come here. I was waiting for you,' Clem said.

'What have you done to her?' Aaron yelled and went to check Destiny. She had dozed off. Aaron tried to wake her up. He slapped on her face, 'Des! Wake up, Des!'

'She won't wake up for now.'

'What did you do to her?' he yelled at Clem.

She didn't respond. She went out to the hall. Aaron took his phone and called Karu's phone. It said not reachable. Cara went into the forest already.

'Damn!' he came out from the room, 'Tell me, what you did?'

'Just her own medication, Aaron. Don't worry. She will be alright. Little high dose won't do any harm,' she sat on the table with a thick coffee solute in water, 'Come on, we need to talk. We shall take care of Destiny later.'

'If anything happens to her, then I will_' Aaron warned her walking towards the table. He didn't know what to say and what to do. 'How did this all happen? Why? Why did you involve her in this?'

'I didn't, Aaron. You did,' she placed the star-shaped pendant on the table. She sipped her coffee. Her face disliked the taste.

Aaron sat on the chair and took the pendant, 'How did you get this?'

'The night I was thrown out of my own ship, I nearly died. You don't know how hard it was to live again. But I survived. I went to the place where the crash had happened. I couldn't find any traces of my ship. I tried to contact that stupid, Phrix. He was not responding. But I felt a presence there. What I wanted in this exploration.' She took another sip and felt nauseated.

'And the only thing I could find there was this pendant. I didn't know how it got there. But I could sense where it came from. This had a strong emotional connection. I visited here that night. I took her shape and made her sleep. Till now, she is sleeping.'

She leaped into the cup, 'Then I went to her office and literally touched everyone on her floor. I was tired of reading memories. It was useless. They all were cussing me for no reason. When I was coming back, I saw you. I should have read one more person. That is you.' She hesitated to drink the coffee anymore.

'If you dislike it why are you drinking it?'

'Because of the form I have now. I have her taste buds too. And her brain stems.' She shrieked, 'Ugh! Living in this girl's body is sick. I'm weak, lonely, and a drug-addicted. I hate her. Her mind has nothing in it. The fastest mind I ever read. Although it has some deep secrets.'

Aaron recalled. 'But you said about her past. Do you know?'

'Oh, yes. I came to discover it later. I'm the only person who knows what she was. Her parents weren't so close to her. Until 17, she was raised by her grandfather, an astrologer in his village. He found that their family psychic sense is within her. He taught her everything he knew. She was happy in the village. That was her golden time.'

'Tell me more.'

'After her grandfather's loss, Des went to live in a school dorm. There she couldn't make friends easily. She was alone, depressed about her grandfather's loss, and the same like that she suffered during college years. The only friends she could make were a hippie gang. She hung out with them. Took all the drugs they could get for her. Actually, she was fine then. She could sleep in peace. But reality didn't favour her.'

'The main reason she lost her memory wasn't an accident. Her parents lied to her. It was due to heavy dosage of drugs. A lot more than I have given her now.'

'After her treatment, she doesn't remember anything. Her friends were scared of being accused. They abandoned her. Even her boyfriend. What an ass-head he was?'

Aaron looked at Des sleeping in her room. He couldn't imagine the life she had once. And wondered how she fixed her life?

'Last time she took her medication a little high. Because her body wanted it like this caffeine, she is now fond of it. Then you know, she lost her memory again.'

She swigged the last of the coffee and spat back into the cup. 'You hope when she opens her eyes, she would have forgotten me. Or if she forgets you and all, which would me more helpful for you.'

Aaron turned back to Clem, 'What do you want from me? Why did you come here before me? Don't you know where the ship is? You want to know from _'

'I know about the boulder. I can go now and kick out Cara and take off with your Karu. That was my plan before seeing you. But now I don't want that, Aaron. I need you on my side.'

'Why?'

'When I read you, I understood something. You and I are the same people, Aaron,' her eyes gleamed on him, 'We have our own veracities. We are not evil. We are just unpredictable. I need you in this battle, Aaron.'

'Why should I help you? A few hours ago, you tried to run a car over me!'

'I didn't mean to do that, Aaron. I cannot hurt even if I want to. Because Destiny won't hurt you. That's something that makes it easy for me to talk with you. And what do you think about Cara? Are you dreaming she will give Karu back to you and let you live peacefully?' She chuckled. 'She will take Karu from here. That's her plan.'

'You are the worst actor I have ever seen. It's clear you are manipulating me. Cara is my friend. And she cares about Karu.'

'Really? Aaron, I read her mind. I know what she did to Karu. She lied to you. The cryopod can heal one within minutes. But she doesn't know anything about that. I bought that from a different place that is totally alien for her. Now, she needs me to heal her. She needs to fix Karu and take her with us.'

'You are lying. I strongly believe Cara.'

'Are you sure? I don't have any need to lie. She has to, Aaron. She is a failure in her life. She is clueless and not so good at acting. This mission is not a choice for her. It's her only chance to live again.'

'Karu is getting healed.'

'Are you sure? She didn't let you open it. Did she?' Clem held Aaron's hand, 'Remember the time she laid Karu inside. Your wounds were healed within seconds. It was the same process. Karu could have been healed instantly. She lied to you. Don't be a fool, Aaron. Remember the last time you saw Karu.' Everything flashed in front of him. The Starship, the cryopod, the flower vase. Karu was hardly breathing. Her wounds remained the same. It didn't look like healing.

'No! No! This can't be happening.'

Clem lit a cigarette and puffed the smoke, 'Aaron, have you ever wondered what these people want in life? Even they don't know. But we know what we need. We are not unstable, unreliable, and frail like them. And they, out there are dangerous.'

'What are you saying? What happened to Karu?'

'She is not healing. She is just kept alive. That only will last for five days, which ends tonight. Maybe, Maybe Cara is trying to heal her. But she needs me for that. She knows that one wrong move in that process can end your girlfriend's life.' She smashed the cigarette on the table.

'Aaron, I don't want anything from you. Just be on my side. I will make your life peaceful again. You will not lose anything. You will get back Karu if you come with me. Only I can save her now.' She waited for his response.

Aaron was confused. He couldn't take things happening around him. His mind had only one thought on the top that is to save Karu.

Clem shrieked, 'Oh! What? You make deals only with Cara?'

Aaron checked his back seat before he started the engine. Destiny was lying unconsciously on the backseat of the car. Clem stepped inside the car and sat on the passenger seat.

'Do we need to take her?' he asked.

'Just a collateral, Aaron. She will be okay. Let's move now.'

— Chapter Twenty-Two —

It was around midnight; the streamside was calm. Cara was in a starship and she heard the noise of the car. She wiped her face and opened the door. She saw Aaron rushing into the ship, holding Destiny on his shoulders.

'What are you doing?' he asked on seeing the cryopod open.

'Karu is healed, Aaron. She needs more sleep. Let her sleep as long as she sleeps. She will be conscious in a day or two. What happened to her?'

'I found Destiny in her apartment. She has overdosed on her medication. I don't know what to do. So, I brought her here.'

Cara came to them. 'Come on, let her lie here. I will look.'

Aaron let her rest on the table and checked on Karu. He looked at her face. He touched her cheeks. He could feel her alive. There were no wounds.

'The wounds were there in the morning. How did she heal all of sudden?'

'What?'

'When did the healing process start? Tell me the truth.'

'I just did it now. It needed time.'

'You are lying to me. From the beginning. You could have healed her the night she got injured. You risked her life for your purpose.'

'Aaron. It's not like that,' she walked to the table, 'Don't get confused. I will explain everything after checking Destiny.'

Aaron looked at Karu. He was confused. He recalled the vision when Clem was holding his hand. The vase had sunflowers. But he just had changed in the morning. There should be a lily when he recalled his memory. He turned at the table. Cara went to the table. She didn't know it was Clem lying there.

'Wait! Don't go there,' He yelled to stop her. But it happened in a flash.

Before Aaron realised what was happening, Clem attacked Cara on her head with the jug on the table. She fell and passed out on the floor.

'What did you do to her?' Aaron was alarmed.

'It's nothing to her. I need to act before she reads me.'

'You lied. You manipulated me like Des does to me,' his eyes were drenching. 'I was used.'

She took a breath, 'Yes, Aaron. I needed you. It was a fake memory. So what? We all have our own skills. Haven't we?'

'This is not fair!' he cried out.

'Well, I know that for sure. But I'm sorry for that. And you don't have to worry, Aaron. You will not be here when she opens her eyes.' She smiled, 'Anyway you got Karu. Take it easy, man.'

Aaron tightened his lips. He looked at Cara fainted out like a corpse chalked around in the traffic. Aaron stood there like some pedestrian who didn't even think to call an ambulance.

'Now our deal is closed,' he motioned her to stop, 'I will take Karu. You leave this place.'

Clem didn't say anything, she just shrugged. She lifted Cara and took a root to tie her hands.

Aaron lifted Karu in her arms. He walked to the door. More than Karu, it was the heavy guilt that he lifted. *I knew it was a manipulation. But where did I lose my mind? I have always doubted Cara. I felt like she would cause harm to Karu. I didn't believe her. It was my fault. I betrayed her. She was a good friend to me. Cara means friend.*

'Now, where is that Phrix?' Clem searched around.

Aaron spotted Phrix before him. He stopped at the stool. He bent down and pretended to adjusting Karu's hair and dress. He whispered, 'I'm sorry. This is me. I don't deserve a friend like her.' He raised up and lifted Karu. He came out and walked to the Car. His tears fell on Karu. He put her in the back seat beside Destiny.

This could be the first meet for both of them. But they were not in a state to acknowledge it. Aaron looked at both for a moment. This meet would be different if Des came to his engagement, he would have introduced her to Karu. Or if he brought Karu to the café where they hang out, he would have introduced Karu to Destiny. He felt guilty for not introducing them to each other before. And then, he decided to do that soon. He promised himself.

'Hey! Wait!' Clem yelled and came to stand on the other side of the car. She smirked at him.

'What?' he said with the lump in his throat, 'What do you want?'

'Nothing. I would like to make a new deal with you. Yeah, I have changed my mind. I'm sorry, this is me. I can't go empty-handed. I hope you understand that. So, I need one of the sleeping beauties,' she gestured at the girls generously, 'You can choose anyone you want.'

'No, that's not what we decided before coming here,' He was freaked out.

'Come on, Aaron, are you going to marry them both? I know you have already chosen Karu. That is a wonderful decision. Let me take Destiny. No one will come to search for her. You know it is her wish too. To go to the stars. Okay?' She opened the door.

'No!' he urged to the other side, 'I won't let you touch her!' he cried out.

'Aaron!' she snorted, 'You know I can just smack you off and take both of them. Leave the way.'

Clem took Destiny. Aaron stood there once again as the pedestrian who doesn't give a shit. He looked at Destiny's face. He reminded her, saying the last time they met, "You are the only friend I ever made, Aaron. In my memory."

He cried, 'Why are you doing this?'

Clem stopped and replied, 'You are so weak, Aaron. Go and live your life.'

—— Chapter Twenty-Three ——

Karu's temperature was high all night. She was shivering in the cold. Aaron didn't know what to do.

The good thing is he didn't stand there doing nothing. He made hot water on the stove and gave her a bedbath. He removed her blood-stained clothes and wrapped her with his coat and the bedsheets available there. He placed a wet cloth on her forehead.

He rubbed her palms between his, 'Don't worry, Karu. Everything will be alright. You will be healed soon. We are going to live a new life.'

After her palms got warm enough. He let her sleep. He stared at her face looking for responses. He didn't even know if it was right to keep her in the cabin for the night. He didn't have any possible reason for what happened to her to say in the hospital. She looked fresh. He believed in Cara's words. She might need sleep.

'Wake up soon, Karu. I want to tell you many things. We are engaged. Our families like each other. We all are one family now. There is a life waiting for you when you open your eyes. The life you always dreamed. Open your eyes soon.'

Her shivering had reduced. Aaron laid next to her spooning over her bed sheets and tried to grasp the heat from her body to his.

He breathed her hair, 'Karu, please open your eyes. I need to see them. I'm in the darkest state ever. Only you could light me up.'

He was scared. Scared of darkness like a child. The darkness of guilt. He wanted someone to say what he did earlier was the only thing anyone could do in his place. But he knew Karu wouldn't say that.

'You should say something, Karu. Tell me what I should do now.'

In the early morning, Aaron took his car and drove to the highway. He bought some paracetamol and a few antibiotic tablets. He shopped for warm clothes for Karu. He drove back quickly with a loaf of bread, buns, and butter for Karu if she feels hungry when she wakes up.

But she didn't wake up when he came back. He ate buns to fill his stomach and washed down with hot water he kept heating.

He changed Karu's clothes. He dissolved the tablets and poured them into Karu's mouth and made her swallow them. She coughed and went back to sleep.

Aaron kept checking Karu's temperature with an electronic thermometer he bought. It was decreasing slowly. He kept wiping her sweat and made a bed bath twice in the day. In the evening, she came to the normal temperature.

Aaron came to the front porch and looked at the trees. The forest remained the same. It has no day or night. He could sense that the starship hadn't left the place yet. In his deep mind, he wished them to go away soon. Before he does anything stupid.

How am I going to live with this?

He heard movements in the bush beside him. He heard the a strange noise. He spotted a reflection of a pair of green eyes.

A wild animal jumped out of the bush. Aaron fell back on the porch floor. He sat up quickly and studied the animal. It was a Fennec fox. A small one. It sniffed on him.

'Hey, what do you want?' Aaron threw a bun to the fox. It sniffed first and started to eat it. 'Huh, you look friendly.'

'Come on. Why are you alone?'

He bonded with a fox within a few minutes. He brushed on its furs. It was fluffy, white, and had a pink nose. It had a pair of long ears. Also, intelligent. It could understand what he said. And he found it was a female.

He spoke to her, 'Do you like me? Please don't like me. I'm not a good person. I have seen terrible things in a week. It was a tough week although I can't be friends like you.'

He started to confess. 'Do you know something?'

The fox listened to him.

'I was not a good boyfriend, not a good son, or a brother either, but was a good friend until last night. I had two friends. They believed me. They called me the only friend they made in this world. I'm the one who knows their secrets. But now, I'm the worst friend ever. The worst, selfish, arrogant human on the planet. I feel shame to even bend my head down. One day, I may betray this motherland too.'

He gazed at the woods, 'Soon she will find where Phrix is and leave this place. She will take my two best friends. One of them belongs to be here. On earth. I'm worried about what will happen to her. But what shall I do? Tell me?'

The fox slanted her head and looked at him. That innocent face tungstened an idea into his mind. 'You wait here. I will come.'

He walked to the bed. He was nervous. He dragged a wooden chair and sat beside Karu.

'You know what Karu?' He took a slice of bread and opened the butter can. He scooped butter with a knife and spread it on the bread. 'I can't do this. I can't be like me anymore. I don't want to. I know I can't live with this guilt forever. How could I lose the people who believed me and live a good life with you?'

'And I'm sure you would tell me this when you wake up.'

He closed the bread with another and placed them on a plate. 'I don't know if I will come back if I go there now. But I have decided now whatever happens to me, I don't want to be the same person who you saw at the cliff when you open your eyes.' He checked if the water was clean and closed the lid. A dinner was prepared for Karu if she wakes up.

He wiped the butter on the knife with a towel. 'I may be bad at everything I was. But I'm a keeper. I have never failed on a promise.' He cut his wrist with the knife. Blood was shedding from his hand, 'As I promised, you should see me as a new person when you wake up. Or else you should not.'

'It is nearly a day. Tell me where Phrix is!' Clem was walking on the ship, yelling at Cara whose hands were tied to the back.

'I told you. It ran away.' Cara replied, sitting on the frightened stool.

'Where did you learn this? Why couldn't I read your memories? When I come to read you are playing movies to me. And they are not even good movies!' Clem scowled at her.

Cara laughed, 'We should do this often, my old friend.'

'Tell me, Cara. I have searched for it all night. I looked all over the streamside. I know it would not go far.'

'Then call it. Does it belong to me?'

'Ugh! I'm going to kill you!'

'Yeah, kill me. Even if you found Phrix, you cannot leave this place. It has lost your trust. You need me now.'

'Seriously? These things are happening to me?'

'Listen to me. Leave this girl here. I will help you to find Phrix. It will show up if I call.' She gestured to Destiny who was lying on the table. 'Why do you want to do this? She has a life here, Clem.'

'I too have a life,' she yelled, 'Did you know that when you pushed me out in the sky? I had survived. I don't want to relive my life as pathetic as you. I took this mission and almost died for that. Now I will complete it.'

'I know it was my fault. I didn't want to do that to you. But please, let's settle this between us. Leave her to Aaron. We will go for another exploration.'

'Don't play smart_' Clem turned to the doorway; Aaron appeared there, standing with the fox in his hands. She scowled at him, 'What are you doing here?'

'I found Phrix near the cabin.' He showed up the fox.

Clem was happy to see that. She came to Aaron and pulled his cheeks, 'You did a wonderful job, Aaron. Now, that's my boy.' She took the fox in her hands. 'Why did you turn into this creature, Phrix?'

Aaron's eyes met Cara. He was too guilty to face her. Cara was confused about what he was trying to do.

'Hey, I got injured while catching Phrix. Shall I use that squid in the tank?' He asked Clem. She threw a doubtful look at him, 'There aren't any medical facilities nearby. I'm bleeding.'

She glanced at the cut on his wrist, 'Do whatever you want. And stay away from her.' She warned him not to go to Cara. 'Phrix! You are back. Do you know how long I was searching for you?' She tried to compromise with the fox.

Aaron fished the wound-eater from the tank and healed himself. This time he couldn't feel any pain. Cara kept eyeing him.

Both of their eyes met. Karu's eyes spoke to him wordlessly. She asked him what was happening. He kept an awkward face. Because he didn't have a plan. Cara was about to ask then why he came here. But she found herself rotating slowly.

The stool on which she sat turned itself to listen to Clem talking with the fox. Cara tried to turn it back. But it was refusing. She pushed it to the other side but it turned back to Clem.

'Look, Phrix. I know I hurt you. But I didn't mean to do it. It is all because of her. Before she came, we used to be together all the time. Remember? I'm your mother.'

The stool slowly moved to Clem. Aaron was terrified to see that. Cara was frightened and pushed herself on it, whispering, 'No, No, No! Stay!'

The stool chirped.

Clem turned at them. She grasped the stool moving. She gasped and shrieked, 'Phrixxx!'

Aaron took off the squid and threw on Clem. It stuck on her face and blinded her. She squeezed the fox in her hands. The Fox screeched and started attacked her with its nails. Phrix stopped moving on seeing the rumble.

Aaron rushed to release Cara. He pulled the root. It was too strong to pull off. Cara yelled at him, 'Leave me! Take Destiny and get out of this place. GO!'

Aaron ran to take Destiny in his arms. He lifted her and ran out from the ship. The fox escaped from Clem's hands and followed him.

'Phrix, move!' Cara commanded the stool. She moved it toward Clem. She squatted and leaned on her hands. Then she slipped her legs through her arms to get her hands in the front. Clem took off the squid from her face. She searched for Destiny and Aaron. She rushed out.

Cara jumped on her back before she reached the doorway. She locked her neck between her wrists with the root. She pulled her back. 'Phrix! Take off! Now.'

Cara used all her energy to pull her back. Clem was stronger. In fact, Destiny is stronger than Karu. So, Cara couldn't hold her for long.

Clem lifted Cara from the back and slammed her through the doorway. Cara fell out on the grass. She screamed in pain. The root on her hands had ripped. Clem jumped from the ship. 'Now, I don't have any reasons to let you live!'

The engine roared directly at Clem.

Aaron ran the car over Clem. She jumped over and hit the windshield. She was thrown away into the stream. Aaron checked on Destiny in the passenger seat. She was safe under the seat belt. He got out of the car. He helped Cara to stand up. She said, 'I'm okay. I told you to get out of this place.'

Clem raised from the water. Rage was burning in her eyes. She walked to the land all ready for the battle. It was more than a battle of good versus bad. It was like compassion versus greed. The vengeance versus the survival. Although it is a two versus one, the minority is stronger.

Cara asked Aaron, 'Do you have any other idea?'

'I'm clueless.'

— Chapter Twenty-Five —

They were fighting for more than an hour. Mostly Cara and Clem. Aaron tried to help her. But got kicked out by Clem.

When you get a chance to wish to a star on your birthday you should ask wisely. I wished to alienate my girlfriend. But I didn't mean it that way. Now within a week, my life was clinging on the edge to save my friends. This could get worse. This could go anywhere from here. This could lead to catastrophe. But it hasn't happened yet. At least I can try.

He got injured the second time. Then he was sitting on the ground holding his paining jaws in one hand. And his elbow was injured. He watched them moving fast and tackling each other. For a moment he forgot who they were and looked at Karu and Destiny fighting.

Oh, crap! I know I wished to see two aliens fighting each other. But not like this. These are the forms of two important women in my life. But now they are like vigilantes. They both knew each other's moves. And they both know if one of them gives up even for a second the other will finish off. Clem is faster. She knows when I come near to her. It's all the same shit again. It's me. I'm the shit. I'm just standing here like I have nothing to do. I'm not a cheerleader to sit here and watch the show. I will go again.

Cara got her chance. She punched Clem on her face thrice. But Clem acted quickly with a head kick. She climbed on Cara and pushed her feet on her. Cara was thrown away.

Aaron walked to Cara, 'You guys don't bleed?' He lifted Cara, 'I'm trying to help you. But I can't do anything.'

'It's my battle, Aaron. Take Destiny and leave this place.'

He shook his head, 'I'm not leaving you like this. You got any clue?'

'I need to hit the back of her head. It is this body's weakness. Remember how I passed out when_' they both were embarrassed to speak out how Aaron betrayed her.

'I'm sorry about that.'

'Are you taking a break?' Clem was swinging her hands and calling them energetically.

Is this a game for her? Aaron thought.

'Hey!' Aaron urged Cara, 'You remember the imposter game?'

'What is about that now?'

'We need to switch cards now. Distract her.'

Cara nodded at him. She walked back to the battle. She ran and tackled Clem's hips. But Clem pushed herself on the ground and remained still. She lifted Cara and threw her on the ground.

Aaron climbed on a blounderstone behind him. He reached the top and there was a rock on it. He tried to lift it. It looked like it had been there for many years. 'Come on, it is just a stone.'

In the past few years, I wanted to lift rocks, ever since Karu said that would make me worthy to get her. I had never tried this before. I had lifted weights. But this is different. So it's a call of a situation I had prepared myself for.

He pushed himself hard and lifted the bottom in his hands. He could feel his muscles tearing apart. He lifted from his side. He flipped it like flipping tyres. And the rock rolled to fall on the ground. It shook the ground and rolled from the boulder. It rolled to Clem.

Clem saw that coming. She moved quickly. The rock hit Cara. It ran over her. Aaron was shocked to see this. 'No, it should not happen!' He screamed and rushed to Cara.

Clem was shaken to see Cara motionless. She went to check on her. She was breathless. She touched her. Her mind was totally blank. Aaron went to take Cara. Clem pushed him back. She scowled 'She's dead.'

Aaron fell on the ground. 'No, she can't be.'

Clem was in a bit of shock. She really didn't want Cara to be dead. She regretted letting it happen. She regretted her arrival to this planet. She hated this place and the people from the beginning. She wanted to go back. But she wanted to go back with Cara. She tried to listen to her heartbeats. There was only calmness left. She couldn't save Cara even if she used the cryopod.

She looked at Aaron in confusion. Her rage was transformed on him. She wanted to leave the place. But she didn't want to leave that place without destroying it. She wanted Aaron to be dead. She wanted to burn this whole forest before she leaves.

'Look what you've done, Aaron.' She walked to Aaron.

Aaron raised up and Clem slapped him to fall on his knees. She yelled at him, 'I told you to go and live your life, Aaron. I didn't want to hurt you. Just because you are like me.'

'She didn't listen to me. She didn't even get the chance to say her last words.' She was biting his teeth and controlling her rage on him. She knew it wouldn't take much to finish him. 'Now you tell me, if you have any last words.'

Aaron was shaking, 'I don't want to be you. I'm not you!' He screamed. 'Maybe I was like you. I didn't care about people. I thought earning money and fame could fix everything. But I was wrong. I might be living like that if she doesn't happen to me. She showed me who I was. Who I was when no one is looking at me. Now I have changed. And she is a good friend I earned.'

'She was my friend too. I know her better than you. You let her die.'

'No, you don't. You don't know. You were wrong about her.' He was wheezing, raised above, and stood on his foot. Clem clenched her fist. Aaron said, 'She… Is a… Terrific actor!'

Cara hit Clem on the back of her head with her elbow. She fell on the ground.

Chapter Twenty-Six

Aaron was waiting on the meadows for Cara. The place was not like he came there for the first time. A storm had passed through the streamside and wiped the calmness it had for years. Beside him, the fox was sitting on the top of the stool. They both like to bond with each other. Cara walked out from the ship.

'Is she okay?' he asked.

'She will be. I had put her into the pod. And when she wakes up, we will not be here. That's good for all of us.' She stood before him.

'So? Are you leaving?'

She nodded and looked at the stool. 'Phrix, return to the ship.' It turned to Aaron.

'Take care, buddy. Don't be scared of anything. You are braver than you think.' He took the fox and left it on the ground. The stool hovered to the ship.

'Can't you stay here? We can adjust things.'

'No, Aaron. That's not good for the environment. Our deal is closing here. You kept my secret and I returned Karu to you. I'm sorry for the crusades you faced.'

'No, I'm sorry. I betrayed you.'

'That is okay. I know you would come back. At least for Destiny.'

'But I came for you too.'

Cara had an awkward silence. She was glad. She had zero anger on Aaron for what he did.

'Thanks, I'm glad I made a friend like you.'

Aaron nodded, 'I hope you will find more friends. And the part you said didn't sound stupid. You can start from there. Give it a try.'

She nodded and took off the ring from her finger. The traces of Mehndi were still on her hands. 'Take care of Karu. If you ever make her cry again, I will crash the ship on you.' She handed him the ring.

They both smiled. They don't know how to make this goodbye special. She moved forward. He thought it was a hug. But she went to his ear, whispering something.

Aaron realized that. 'Thank you.'

She nodded, 'Goodbye, Aaron.' She walked back to the ship. She didn't bring anything while she came here. But now, she was taking the form of the girl he loved.

After this, he cannot meet her again. She came as a spare for his girlfriend. Now returning as his best friend.

She went into the ship. It closed. It was looking like just a boulder which is not. It was a big flying rock. Like a video playing in reverse, a space rock hovered up from the ground and floated in the air.

Aaron looked up at it from the ground. It blazed away in a blink. The sky went clear. The place came back to normal. The crickets started to sing.

What Aaron didn't notice in that place was the new varieties of weeds and flowers bloomed on the place where the ship was.

In fifty years, a cocoon will burst and a new species of butterfly which can swim underwater will come out. It will lead to an evolution on earth which will happen after a million years. But for now, it is a new normal.

Aaron drove to Destiny's apartment. He lifted her and walked to the stairs. His hands ached because of lifting the heavy rock. He badly wanted to sleep. He saw her coming back to consciousness. She blabbered something. Aaron made her lean on him and tried to open the door.

The neighbour's light turned on and the woman who he met last night peeked from her door. He felt a little embarrassed to hold destiny like this. He opened the door and took her inside.

He laid her on her bed and spread the bed sheet over her. She opened her half eyes and looked at him. 'Aaron?'

'Shhh… You are alright. Sleep. I will come and meet you in the morning.' He turned off the bedside lamp and walked out from the loft. When he walked out two more neighbours were eying on him.

—— Chapter Twenty-Seven ——

-     Hi, Aaron. I'm sorry if I'm disturbing you.

    Can we meet?

Aaron received a text message from Destiny in the morning. He replied. They decided to meet at the café.

Destiny arrived at the cafe on her red scooter. She parked behind Aaron's car and locked her helmet on it.

She entered the café and climbed the stairs to the rooftop area. There she spotted Aaron, sitting on the open café table, waving at her. She made a smile and sat in front of him.

Aaron noticed changes in her. Her face was plain. It didn't have any make up or morning glow. It had a plain look that couldn't be wiped off. Her eyes were swollen from the long sleep. She tied her hair to a ponytail. 'Hey... You look so...'

'Beautiful?'

'No.' He was confused about her deadpan behaviour. But he could feel the real Destiny. 'Yes!' He shook his head, 'Maybe!'

'You are saying all the answers. Are you alright?'

'I'm good. How are you feeling? You look tired.'

'I'm not tired. I feel good now. Maybe I was pissed off for a week, I think.'

The café' owner placed two coffees on the table and grinned at them. They both smiled at her and she left.

'Do you have any problem?'

'Aaron, I want to talk to you,' she added two sugar cubes and stirred her coffee.

'I need to tell you something before you say_'

'Mine is important. Let me speak! I actually don't know what is happening in my life. It happened again,' she spread her arms like it was the big bang that happened again to her, 'I knew something like this would happen. But it is different this time. I'm feeling confused. I'm... I don't know if I have ever experienced this feeling before. It's new and killing me.'

'What happened again?'

'The memory loss. I don't remember anything that happened in the past week,' She spoke seriously and bent over to him, 'Last Sunday, I was looking at the moon through my telescope. Then tonight I woke up in the middle and looked at the moon. The phases had passed. I was freaked out to find the alignment of stars had changed. Then I checked the calendar.'

Aaron listened to her to know her side of the story.

'I have skipped time. I forgot what I did this week. Then I checked my medication. I had consumed too much,' she shrunk her face, 'And, Aaron, I'm so scared of knowing what I did. I wanted to know that from you. That's why I texted you for this meeting.'

Aaron was surprised to see things falling in place. He didn't have to explain anything to her now. He thought *the more ignorance she has, the safer she is.*

'The last thing I remember was before going to bed, I tried to call you to wish for your birthday. But I couldn't get you in line.'

He cleared his throat, 'I had gone out of the city. It was a family trip.'

'Oh, did I wish you?' She asked.

'Yes! You did. In the morning.'

'I'm glad I did. Or else I would regret this.' She felt relieved and sipped her coffee.

She remembers my birthday. She tried to wish me. This means she is worthy! But what happened to her energy? She looks puzzled. It was all my fault. I wish I could take care of her. I should.

She made the 'Mmm…' sound she always does while drinking coffee. Aaron was pleased to hear this. Aaron had seen Cara as Karu a few times. But he could never see Clem as Destiny. Because Destiny can't be defined with her looks. There are many other things that make her Destiny. He wanted to make sure he hadn't harmed her with any post-trauma.

He leaned forward, 'Are you okay now? Can we go to the hospital? Or shall we check with a neurologist? I know someone. It will be private.'

'No, it happens in life,' Destiny was in her element. She smiled and took life as a humorous book, 'Not in anyone's life. But for me, it's a part of my life.'

'This morning when I went out, my neighbours saw me differently. They don't want to talk to me. I don't know why. Remember my vanishing plan? To get rid of this city without leaving any information to the company and no contact with colleagues. I thought of it. But then I had this one reason to stay here, in this work and this city.'

Aaron gave his attention, 'What is that?'

'It is what I remembered like a dream. That happened in the past week. Or maybe last night.' She looked directly at him.

'That is you, Aaron. I feel like you were there when I was in trouble. The dream was like you saved my life. You are the saviour of my insecurity. I feel like... Like...' she closed her eyes and inhaled her breath and exhaled her words, 'I think, I love you, Aaron.'

Aaron was not there mentally.

'I know I'm freaking you out! It is too soon between us. What am I doing?' She shook her head.

'It's up to you now. What do you think of me? I know I'm not an alien to you. I'm your type. And I thought you would think the same. Aren't you?'

She found him disturbed. 'Aaron? Are you crying?'

Aaron's eyes were ponded. He spoke weepingly. Destiny couldn't understand any sentence he tried to convey. She was confused. Aaron was not like this when she lastly met him. She didn't know his emotional barricade was already open. She tried to crack the sentences. The overall moral she got from his speech was that he was already in love with someone. She was chaotic about why he got so emotional to say that. She stopped him straining to speak.

'Aaron, it's okay. Relax.'

'Calm down. I just asked... I'm sorry, I don't know that you are committed to someone. You haven't told me before. And I'm not serious. I just asked what I thought.'

He nodded at her. 'It's my fault. I should have told you.'

'Fine, now I'm cleared. I am happy that you are in love. That girl is so lucky to have you in her life. Forgot what I said earlier. Are we okay?'

'Yes, we are.' He pulled the tears not to fall down.

'Good. So... that's it. I have no reason to not vanish.'

'Please don't do this.' The tears fell. He wiped.

'Sorry, Aaron. It's time to say goodbye,' she stood up, 'Do you want something else? Another coffee?'

'No, it's enough.' he looked at his untouched coffee.

'Okay, I'll pay and leave. Take your time. You are the best friend I ever had, Aaron,' she smiled and waved him good-bye, 'I hope I won't forget you.'

Aaron cried. Cried emotionally and something had awakened within him. When Destiny said she loved him, he went back to the time Karu said, "I love you" for the first time. The voice he heard in himself when he saw the text message.

Now I understand everything. I understand that I love Karu more than anything. No one can replace her in me. I want to be with her. I want to cry on her lap and confess everything to her.

'Oh my gosh!' A person gasped on seeing Aaron crying in the café. He was embarrassed to look up. The café was usually a crowded one. Because as Destiny said this is where the best coffee in the city is available. It's the Sherlins Café.

He wiped his tears. His reddish eyes met the person. It's the café owner Simeela throwing him shocked look.

'Did you guys break up?' Her eyes almost filled with tears. She couldn't take that as someone else's problem. She felt worried that she couldn't see them together anymore, 'Are you okay, Aaron?' She clasped her hands together. 'You want anything else?'

'I'm more than okay.' He smiled, nodding at her, 'I have never been better than this,' he grasped his car key.

—— Chapter Twenty-Eight ——

The car dinged on the sidewalk of the highway. It was a call from Karan. Aaron attended and spoke to the microphone on his steering wheel. 'Hey, Karan… how are you doing?'

'Wh… where is Karu?' he urged in his malicious tone.

Aaron took it cool. 'Uh… She's around here. Anything important?'

'It has been three days since she left the house. No calls, no messages. What are you both thinking? You two are not married yet. You are just engaged, okay? I can stop this from happening anytime.'

'Come on, buddy, we are brothers-in-law now. And Karu is safe here with me. You know today is her birthday. She would be happy to celebrate with me. Don't worry. I will drop her at your house in the morning. And when I come there… We shall speak. With some drinks and chilling out with a movie? Huh? What do you say? You can choose the film for now.'

There was an awkward silence for a while.

'Take care of Karu.' Karan cut the phone call.

Aaron grinned and slid down the glass of the car window. A salesman from the bakery handed him a box of cake, 'Thank you so much,' he paid him with cash and refused the balance with a smile.

He started the car and drove as slow as he could for the cake. Even people on the sidewalk could walk faster than him. The smile was still on his face. The meeting with Destiny had awakened him.

Destiny. She has taught me something. She doesn't know what her life was. But I know. Life is weird, also beautiful. It's nothing wrong with who we were. It is all about what we have changed in ourselves.

Guiltiness is overrated. It makes us weak. To hate ourselves. It sucks out all the hope we had. The good deeds we did in life seem to us like nothing in the moment one is in guilt. I mean, if you can't forgive yourself, then who will?

The second chance. It's not easy to get in one's life. If we get it, we should use it as Destiny does. Luckily, I got one. And I will make most of it. The Aaron, who was here in the past week, is not here.

I'm saying this for the second time, you don't know what life can bring you within a week. A few years ago, I told Karu that I love her. Within a week she told me that she loves me too. That has changed my whole life.

Last week, it was my birthday, and now it's Karu's. Everything in me has changed. My life has changed. And the special thing is it doesn't matter whatever changes, Karu is still with me. All the time.

What would it be if I lost Karu? In any timeline or any dimension or even in a thought? That Aaron would be the most miserable person in the universe. Gladly, I'm not him.

Aaron reached the cabin. He parked the car and took out the cake box. He walked to the cabin, lifting his head at the stars.

And when it comes to friends, some friends are like the street lamps while we drive on a highway, they light us and pass us soon. But some friends are very far away and still light up on us. Distance doesn't matter. They are there for us all the time, like these stars.

At 10 pm, Aaron noticed Karu's eyeballs were moving after almost 48 hours of sleep. He went close to her, 'Karu, wake up. Open your eyes.'

She opened them. The eyes of the darkest and loudest oceans. Aaron's pilgrimage was over on seeing those. That was enough for all the struggles he had faced.

'Aaron?' She got up and looked around. She noticed her new dress. It was a purple gown Aaron bought for that day.

'What happened? Why am I here?' She touched her face, shoulders, arms, and hips as if she was checking whether everything's at place or not.

'Hey… Hey… don't be scared. Look at me. Aaron here. Nothing happened. We are here in the cabin. Look.' He checked her head for wounds. There was no trace of the injury. Even the acne marks disappeared and left a few freckles on her cheeks. Her skin was glowing. 'Do you have a headache?'

'No. I'm okay,' she looked confused, 'I feel so new.'

'That's good.'

'What happened?' she recalled her last memory, 'You went to the cliff. And…'

'And you passed out there. Maybe you were scared. But it all happened a week ago.'

'What?' she was alarmed.

'Yes, look at the date,' he showed his mobile, 'It's your birthday tonight, Karu,' he lifted her shoulders, 'Get up and get fresh.'

'What was I doing in a week?' She stood on the ground, 'Why don't I remember anything?'

'What are you saying, Karu?' He ushered her to the restroom, 'A few minutes ago, you said you are having a headache and went to sleep.'

'I don't remember anything,' she spotted the fox in the window, 'What is a fox doing here?'

'Uh… It is a friendly fox.' He handed her a new bamboo toothbrush and paste, 'And are you speaking seriously? You don't know what happened?'

'No, I feel like sleeping for a long time.'

'Are you okay? Shall we go for a medical check-up?'

'No need for now. I'm feeling so good,' she smiled.

'Then it is good.' He leaned on the doorway. Karu started to brush her teeth in front of the mirror above the sink.

'What did I say to my parents before coming here?' she looked at him through the mirror, 'And what happened that night? Did I go home without any doubt?'

Aaron gazed at her brushing teeth. The way she was moving, speaking, rolling her eyes. 'You don't need to worry about that anymore. Also, you don't need to lie to them again. Look at your hand.'

'Whose ring is this?' She asked with foam in her mouth.

'Our engagement rings.' Aaron smiled and showed his ring.

Karu almost choked. She spitted out. 'What??'

Aaron told Karu everything. Everything that happened in the past week. Everything Cara did, he changed them as Karu did. He told her about how she was introduced to his colleagues.

She was surprised by the story. Her face was illuminated by each event that happened in the past week. She was not believing them all until he showed her the photos of their engagement. She was amazed by Cara's dance video and didn't believe that she did those moves.

She could say only one thing, 'It is not me!'

— Chapter Twenty-Nine —

'**H**appy Birthday, my Karuvizhi!' he wished her. They cut the cake and barely eat it. Karu was glowing a lot more with a smile on her face.

After the cake cutting, they were swinging on the front porch. The fox was eating the rest of the cake.

Aaron was gazing at the forest. Karu leaned on his shoulder, caressing his arms. She found he had lost some weight in a week. His eyes had dark circles and were embossed a little. His stomach groaned often. He didn't remember when he last slept or ate well.

'Aaron, I remember something. It is not so clear.'

'What is that?' he asked.

'I'm not sure. It was so dark. I didn't know if my eyes were open or not. I feel like I was meditating. Then I heard your voice. It was so far from me. You were talking to me.'

'Really?' He wrapped his arm over her, 'What I said?'

'You told me that everything will change. You will change. You cried. I was listening to you. I wanted to come to you and hug you. I didn't want you to cry. But I can't reach you. I was floating in some void.'

He hung his head down. 'That was true. I told you all those.'

She got up, 'But why?'

'Because Karu,' he scratched his neck, 'I was not being me, without you. I need you. I need you all the time. That's how Aaron Stitch functions.' He turned to face her, 'You are the one who always cares for me. Even in your sleep. But I wasn't good enough for you.'

'Who told you? You are the best,' she pulled his cheeks.

'No, I wasn't,' he held her both hands, 'After all, I found that I love you more than anything in the world. I love you, Karu. Don't leave me again.'

'Why are you saying all this, Aaron? Where did I go? I know about you. Everyone knows how much you love me. I'm the one who is not worthy.'

'No, Karu. I have to say this now.' He shook his head, tears filled his eyes, 'Everyone knows how much I love you. But no one, even you, doesn't know how much you love me.'

Karu was moved on hearing this.

'That's why I'm saying all these. Everyone should know that I'm nothing without you. I love you, Karu.'

'I love you, Aaron. Don't think too much. Come here.' She hugged him tightly. He held her to his chest and moved his face towards her hair, ear and face.

This warm skin, the scent of Karu, her soft hair. This is everything I missed about her. And her eyes. I was waiting for them to open. Now I can look into them all night. This is Karu. This is my girlfriend.

Wow, her father is an underrated poet, as he named her 'Karuvizhi' which means dark eyes. I never knew when I started to love Karu. It was always her from the beginning and I had wondered many times why it was always her.

Until this moment happens. Looking into her eyes, those dark and round eyes remind me of something. Something happened a few years ago, a memory which I had lost in time.

I remember it like a dream. She was a little teenage girl with double braided hair sitting in front of me. The me who never talked much to her and about her. She was staring at me. I still don't know if she was looking at me or not. But I could see her eyes in the middle of my collywobbles. There was this darkness in her eyeballs. The darkness which fills the universe. And in that universe, I saw a vision of me and her together in a beautiful place with happiness, love, and fortune.

That moment made me fall in love with her. That vision told me that she is made for me. That was the prophecy I saw in her eyes. The signal from the universe.

However, I failed to capture the lesson from it; I kept receiving the lessons. Now, the universe has slapped me in the face with the same lesson and I got it. Now I realize that this is the moment I saw in her eyes. This place, this happiness, this love and fortune we share with each other are what the prophecy I saw in her eyes. She is the one I deserve to love and be loved.

'Why are you looking at me like that?' Karu found it weird, Aaron gazing at her with a grin on his face.

He shook his head, 'Tell me. What do you want for your birthday?'

'What shall I ask?' She pretended to be thinking.

Aaron got what she was doing. She was playing their traditional game. 'Wait for a second, I think you haven't given me what I always ask for my birthdays.'

She pointed out, 'Did you ask this year? I think I remember that far.'

He cleared his throat, 'Well, I was going to.'

'You first!' she ordered.

'Okay, fine,' he got closer to her and whispered, 'Let's share our gifts together.'

They kissed. Aaron tightened his eyelids, holding his tears. He inhaled her breathe. He tasted love in her upper lip between his lips. She was fresh as never before. He touched her tongue and felt like a curse was fading. She was panting when they were apart.

'Hey, I have got something for you.' He took a paper bag he bought from a local hotel.

'What?'

'Finally, I found what your favourite food is.'

'Really? What is that?' She smiled.

He opened the box and showed up to her, '*Idli!* Am I right?'

She laughed when she saw two packages of *idlies*. 'How are you sure about that?'

'Huh… A friend helped me to guess it.'

'Who?' She kept asking questions, 'That colleague you mentioned that day? What's her name?'

'Nah… It's from my guardian angel.' He glanced at the sky. He wished his angelic friend was looking at them. He hoped she was.

'Anyway, today's dinner is idli. And for dessert…' He opened a plastic box, 'Honey candies!'

She burst into a laugh. That was her favourite candy in her childhood. She almost forgot that existed. It brought many memories to her. They both went into their teenage personalities. He took a piece and fed it into her mouth, 'Am I right? Is this your favourite food?' He asked.

'I don't know,' she got excited and jumped to hug him, 'But I really like it. And I like you too… I love you so much.'

—— Epilogue ——

Fifty years had passed. The swimmable butterfly was wandering under the stream water, waiting for someone to discover him and name him.

The 76 years old grandpa, Aaron, could still swim on the south beach of Elysian City with kids. Grandma Karu remained the same person who takes care of bags and shoes on the shore. The melanin level in her body had been reduced. Her eye colour had turned into a tint of brown. Yet she was still a mystery. None of the family knew that she was enjoying the sunset more than them. Time had made them old, wise, and even happy. Time also works in a different way.

Cara was sitting in a restaurant, looking at other diners spurting drinks while laughing at the comedy show playing on the screen. Their laugh gives her hope. Clem was staring at her in the opposite seat.

They were still on their return journey. A waitress came to take their orders. 'Looks like you two went for a trip.'

'Yeah, we went to a planet called Earth. There we tried to kill each other.' Clem smirked at the waitress. 'It was fun.'

That was an awkward answer to hear from a customer. 'I will bring the same you always have.' The waitress left the place.

Cara exhaled, 'You can't do anything now. Let's settle down. What happened on the Earth, stays on the Earth. After we land, you go your way. And I will go mine.'

'Yeah, thanks for making me homeless like you. Now, I don't have anything to sell. The whole exploration was a disaster.'

Cara took the vase of sunflower and gave it to Clem, 'Here, it has different combinations of molecules. You can fill your investment with this.'

Clem shrugged and took it. She looked at the sunflower. She recalled the fake memory she gave to Aaron. She came to know about the flower change.

'It wasn't a fake memory! Was it?' she asked.

'What?' Cara turned from the screen.

'You knew how to heal her instantly. But you wanted her to not heal. And somehow you made her survive again.'

Cara was speechless. Her heart weighed more. The moments she decided to forget came to her mind.

When she met Karu for the first time she felt something. Like the universe had brought her to that place at that time. She felt Karu was dying. She took her shape. But when she found she was alive she knew she had some purpose to live again. Cara wanted to know what Karu's purpose was. She kept her alive and lived Karu's life. She understood many emotions and life lessons from the life Karu was living.

Clem wondered how she got that idea at first, 'I think I got this from that Destiny girl. Wow, I can predict the future from now. The Exploration isn't a waste. So, glad to work with you, old friend.' She spotted tears flowing from Cara's eyes. 'That's weird. Why are you crying now?'

When Cara was at the stream alone, she saw herself as Karu. She liked her body. She decided to keep it even after she returned from the Earth. But when she saw Aaron taking care of her, she wished to be in her place. With her family, with Aaron's family and of course with Aaron.

Clem took a breath. She moved closer to Cara. 'Come on, I could understand you. You loved him. Didn't you? It's not your fault. He hugged you when you first saw him, you both were engaged. Still, you were just a look-a-like of someone who he loved. Now, you got heartbroken.' She sat beside her and grabbed Cara's shoulders. She found something else in her.

That night before Aaron and Clem came to the streamside, Cara was staring at Karu for a long time. She could have let her die as she was going to when she found her. As she decided earlier to live as Karu thereafter. She wished she was emotionless like she was earlier. She wished to have the strength to fight with her heart. Tears pelted on her face. She threw up her chance to let Karu live her life. She started the healing process at the edge of Karu's lifetime. Cara extended it for a long.

'Wait! Did you desire her life?'

Yes, in this vast universe what Cara envied was a life of a regular girl who wants to live a regular life, who has a beautiful family, and a loving husband, who is now looking at her family by the seashore, and who has a name that is adequate for her. The name of the girl is Karuvizhi.

━━━━━ ★★★ ━━━━━

Also from the Author

Art, Text, Love.

This book is dedicated to you. Yes, you. If you love to have coffee when it is raining. If you get excited about seeing a sky full of stars. And if you ever fell in love at first sight with a complete stranger.

"First love isn't something that happens first in life. It can happen even after few love bonds."

Before a monsoon rain starts, Jay, a coffeeholic aspiring writer who works as a reader for blind people in a library, walked in his shoes to have a coffee in his favourite cafe in Castle Town. What he saw in the cafe is a new girl who is a comic artist named Cassy. Is this love at first sight? Maybe, but not between Jay and Cassy. It's a story of Art and Text falling in love with each other.

This book is penned with Jay's beautiful poems in between the story. And his text conversation with Cassy and her comics. So, what are packaged in this book is just Art, Text, Love.

www.ingramcontent.com/pod-product-compliance
Lightning Source LLC
Chambersburg PA
CBHW020330160726
47992CB00004B/1787